Sto

Half a Team

Half a Team

by

Maxine Drury

Decorations by Gerald McCann

LONGMANS, GREEN AND CO.
NEW YORK · LONDON · TORONTO
1960

LONGMANS, GREEN AND CO., INC.
119 WEST 40TH STREET, NEW YORK 18

LONGMANS, GREEN AND CO. LTD.
6 & 7 CLIFFORD STREET, LONDON W 1

LONGMANS, GREEN AND CO.
20 CRANFIELD ROAD, TORONTO 16

HALF A TEAM

PUBLISHED SIMULTANEOUSLY IN THE DOMINION OF CANADA BY
LONGMANS, GREEN AND CO., TORONTO

FIRST EDITION

LIBRARY OF CONGRESS CATALOG CARD NUMBER 60-11977

Printed in the United States of America

For
Donna *and* Bonnie
who helped by being fourteen

Half a Team

1 : Cindy's Team

IT was nearly three hours since Cindy Martin had come home from school, leaping from the bus like a prisoner released. After she had changed her clothes, trading dress and oxfords for overalls and sneakers with the same joyous relief one might expect a caterpillar to find in putting on his butterfly's wings, she had gone to work.

So far, she had fed and watered the chickens and gathered the eggs. She had fed and watered the pigs. She had let the two cows into the barn and milked them, not forgetting to feed Shep, the dog, and the eight white barn cats. She had strained the fresh milk into the stone crocks in the cool, gloomy cellar, and skimmed the morning's cream into its gallon can to save for the creamery. She had fetched fresh milk for supper, skimmed milk for the pigs' morning meal, and brought up the soiled pails, crocks and straining cloths. Then she had filled the lamps from the big kerosene drum in the corner of the shed, fetched wood from the wood-pile for the kitchen stove, and carried in a pail of water from the well.

The outdoor tasks Cindy had performed with a sort of grave enjoyment. The inside ones she had hurried through, and finished with relief. The silence of the big, empty house had made her feel too much alone, and sad. Her own footsteps, the rattling of dishes and pans as she set them down, the ticking of the clock, didn't bring the big house to life at all. They only made the silence seem more heavy, the emptiness more complete.

In the cellar only dim light came through the high, cobwebbed windows. The air was chill and musty. Corners were caves of blackness in which mysterious shapes seemed to move. Cindy had done her work there with her heart pounding hard and slow, her breath almost choked by the lump terror brought into her throat. But if anyone had asked her whether she had been afraid, she would have denied it, and sincerely. Being afraid didn't count unless you ran away, and Cindy Martin had never run away yet. Well, never but once. And she never would again.

These were the jobs Cindy did every evening after school. She always finished them tired, her legs and shoulders aching with lifting and carrying, with walking and climbing. But the job just ahead of her, feeding the horses, was the one she loved. Always before, it had lifted her out of the deepest fatigue. Today the magic didn't quite work.

Walking down from the house to the barn, she had seen her father standing by the watering trough with Ben Thompson. Ben was here often lately, talking to her father in his dry old voice. She had glowered at him as she passed, wishing that the hate in her eyes could be strong enough to drive him away forever. But she knew it wouldn't be. Each time Ben left, Cindy hoped he would never come back. But he always did.

Always when he was here Ben talked about the same

thing. Sometimes he smiled and cajoled, and Cindy's father smiled and shook his head. Sometimes he looked grim, and his voice sounded almost threatening, and Cindy's father still shook his head. Tonight, when Cindy had passed her father, he was still shaking his head. But, for the first time, there was the shadow of indecision on his face.

As she climbed the ladder to the haymow, Cindy tried to persuade herself that she had only imagined that look of indecision. Of course, she told herself, she must have. Her father had said no to Ben dozens of times, and nothing had changed. Nothing had happened that would make him even think of saying yes. Surely it had been only the way the slanting rays of the setting sun put most of his face in shadow, that had given him that sudden look of doubt.

Cindy took the pitchfork that leaned against the wall near the top of the ladder, and began to drag forkfuls of hay across the dusty floor and shove them through the opening beside the ladder. The hay made a soft rustling as it settled into the alleyway below. The pitchfork was taller than Cindy, and its handle, polished by long use, was almost too thick for her small hands to hold. She struggled to load it with the tangled hay, to lug it across the stretch of rough board floor, then to pull it free of its load. Sweat sprang out on her face, and drops ran down to sting her eyes. Dust and chaff filled the air, pricked her nose and throat, and settled itchily on her skin. She panted, sneezed twice, and stopped to wipe her face with her sleeve. Peering down the opening, she decided that the heap of hay was big enough.

Sighing with relief, she propped the pitchfork carefully against the wall. Then she gathered herself together, took a deep breath, and leaped down onto the pile.

The horses turned their heads to look at her. Their pointed ears, alertly forward above their long faces, made them look startled and disapproving. The old mare, Queenie, whinnied impatiently. And no wonder! Here they all were, ready for their meal, and she was sprawled on top of it.

"I'd hate to have you lying on my supper," Cindy told Queenie, as she began to pick up armfuls of hay and fill her manger. Then she had to stop a moment to giggle at the thought of Queenie flopping down on top of a plate of meat and potatoes and gravy. There wouldn't be much left of it for sure! And then there would be the job of getting the mess off Queenie's bright copper-red coat.

Cindy moved on, down the row of mangers. First she explored the left-over hay in the bottom of each, to see if any of the hens had laid eggs there. Then she dumped in hay to fill it to the top.

Next to Queenie there was the bay team, Captain and Jerry, side by side in a big double stall. They were busily cleaning the last of the oats out of their feed boxes. Since they had been working today, they had grain too, not just hay as the others did who had spent their day in the pasture.

Jerry, eager for affection as a baby, rubbed his nose gently against Cindy's shoulder. She stopped for a moment to pat him. Instantly, Captain, with a little squeal of annoyance, reached over and nipped his partner on the neck. Jerry shrank away, and with a look of abject apology began to munch on a wisp of hay.

"Oh! You're mean!" Cindy glared at Captain. She fished two eggs out of a corner of his manger and put them in an empty basket for safekeeping. Then she began to give Captain his hay. Captain tossed his head, and glared at her triumphantly.

Cindy sighed and shook her head. Jerry did so want petting and praising, and she could never resist giving it to him. But Captain would never let him enjoy it. She had tried going to Captain first, so that he wouldn't feel neglected. But it hadn't worked. Captain didn't want petting himself. If she reached toward his nose, he would toss his big head out of reach and roll his eyes so that the whites showed. Yet he didn't seem really frightened or angry. Cindy had decided that it was just that Captain didn't like people, and he resented seeing how much Jerry loved them. Too bad, for both of them, that long ago they had been made a team.

Next to them was the black team, Inky and Sooty. There was one egg, an extra-big one, in Sooty's manger. Cindy took it out and filled the mangers, smiling approvingly at the two black mares. Now, they were a perfect team. Physically, they were a match, almost inch for inch and pound for pound. Their shining coats might have been cut from the same enormous bolt of black satin. Except for the broad white blaze down Inky's face, it would have been nearly impossible to tell them apart.

In disposition, too, they were matched. Sweet, placid, infinitely patient, the two mares worked and ate, rested and grazed together in the pasture, in perfect agreement. Unfortunately, they shared a serious fault. At any unexpected moment, set off generally by some noise or event they had accepted dozens of times before without alarm, they panicked. When that happened, they were instantly transformed into lunatics, so frantic with fear that they were in real danger of killing themselves as well as anyone who happened to be near.

Wedged tightly between Inky's ribs and the wall was Inky's yearling foal. She had been named Stormy because she had entered the world during a week-long spell of wind and driving rain. Stormy was at the awkward age. Tall, and big-boned as a full-grown horse, she had still the long-legged gawkiness of a foal. She followed Inky about like a baby. Yet if Inky gave her the warning nip proper for a foal who is misbehaving, Stormy flared into adolescent defiance. Just now, Stormy was cheekily grabbing mouthfuls of hay from Inky's manger, dragging them over the side, and letting them drop to the floor of the stall. Inky laid back her ears disapprovingly, but did nothing.

Cindy frowned. She scolded, "Stormy!"

Stormy blinked foolishly, and shook her head. Then she took a bigger mouthful, and dropped it after the rest.

This could not be allowed. Hay was to eat, not to waste. Cindy walked sternly to the end of the row of mangers, through the narrow opening between it and the wall, and back past two empty stalls. There was no space between Stormy and the wall, or between Stormy and Inky, to get to Stormy's head.

Cindy studied the situation briefly. Then she said gently, "Whoa there, girls." That was one of her father's rules, one she had heard so often she couldn't forget it. Never walk behind a horse without speaking to him. If he doesn't know who or what you are, you can't blame him for kicking.

With her hand on Inky's side, Cindy walked to the front of the stall and squeezed past in front of her. She shoved Stormy back, one hand on her nose, the other on her shoulder. Stormy stood stubbornly for a moment, then backed up obediently. Cindy shooed her out of the barn and shut the lower half of the door. But Stormy wouldn't go away. She stood with her head over the door, nickering imploringly. Inky ignored her, and got on with her meal.

Now Cindy came to the team she always left until last so that she could give them any extra bits of food or time that were left. This was the white team, her very own. Ever since she could remember, even when she had been so small her father had had to lift her up to let her pat their soft noses, being with them had been pure joy. Now it wasn't.

She looked at the two white horses, and remembered her father's face as she had passed him a little while before. She had worked hard to convince herself that she had imagined its expression of uncertainty. But seeing Tom and Sade made her know that she hadn't imagined it. It had been real. Suddenly she saw their stall empty, and the fear came back, wrenching at her stomach so strongly that for a moment she was afraid she would be sick.

Because what Ben Thompson had wanted, all these times he had come and talked and talked, was her team.

2 : The Seeing Eye

Cindy took a deep breath and clamped her lips tight with determination. There was nothing to be afraid of, and she wouldn't think about it.

She reached into Sade's manger and brought out three eggs. In Tom's her hand hit stickiness and bits of shell. She glared at Tom.

"Tom, you bad horse!" she scolded. "I've told you a million times not to eat our eggs. Besides, you mess up all your nice clean hay." She pulled out the worst of the mixture of hay and eggshells, dropped it to the floor, and then wiped her hands on the legs of her overalls. Her stern expression melted suddenly into a broad grin. "But I suppose that's what makes your coat so nice and shiny," she admitted. "Do you know how pretty you are, you old thief?"

Tom tossed his head high, then lowered it, as if he were nodding in agreement. He seemed smugly assured of his own irresistible charm.

Cindy reached into the pocket of her overalls and brought out two apples. She had picked them up in the orchard next to the chicken yard, especially as a treat for her team. She held one out to Tom. His soft lips plucked it daintily from her hand, and rolled it up be-

8

tween his strong teeth. With eyes half closed, he crunched it in leisurely enjoyment.

Watching him fondly, Cindy thought that Tom must be the most beautiful horse in the whole world. He was slender and graceful. His coat was smooth and soft as white satin, his nose like pearl-gray velvet. His eyes were large and brown, full of light and expression. No wonder Ben Thompson, miserly as he was, wanted to buy him. No wonder he kept coming back time after time to raise his offer.

Turning the remaining apple in her hands, Cindy hesitated. She longed to give it to Tom, but that wouldn't be fair. Sade was his teammate, and mustn't be slighted.

"Here, Sade, an apple for you, too." Cindy tried to make her voice as warm as it had been for Tom, but she couldn't quite do it. She held the apple under Sade's nose and watched her pink lips fumble for a moment and then grasp it, only to drop it again.

Sade lowered her head, exploring the hay in the bottom of her manger. But while she groped, Tom's bright eyes had found the treasure. His head came over the partition and he caught the apple quickly between his teeth. The gleam of triumph in his eyes as he tossed his head high for a moment with the apple between his teeth, made Cindy burst into a sudden laugh of delight.

Tom wasn't only the most beautiful horse in the world, but also the most clever. He took what he wanted—the eggs, Sade's special tidbits—not by ill-tempered force, but with a slyly innocent dexterity. And Sade, poor stupid thing, hadn't even spunk enough to resent his thievery. Instead of turning on him with ears laid back, as any horse of spirit would have done, she only stood still in patient resignation. Her naked pink nose quivered with disappointment, and she blinked her cloudy white eyes stolidly.

Cindy hurried to bring hay and fill the white team's mangers. Sade could at least console herself with hay for being robbed of her apple. Even though Tom would help himself to any particularly tempting wisps, Sade wouldn't grieve about that, for she wouldn't have seen them. Sade had been blind for so long that she had probably forgotten what hay looked like.

The latch clicked. The barn door swung creakingly open. Slanting sunlight streamed in, flat yellow rays filled with dancing dust specks. Dropping the last armful of hay into Sade's manger, Cindy looked into the dazzle of light. Ben Thompson was coming through the doorway, her father following close behind. They stood for a moment, outlined blackly against the brightness. Then her father swung the door closed, and Cindy blinked hard in the sudden darkness. But after a moment her eyes adjusted themselves again, and she could see the two men standing close beside her.

Cindy's heart gave a little jump of pride, as it always did when she saw her father after being away from him for a while. Always, even though she knew him so well and saw him every day, she was surprised at how strong he was. His wiry, compact body seemed solid and indestructible. His gray eyes were cool and steady. He didn't wear the shapeless overalls most farmers used, and his gray pants and blue shirt somehow managed to look neat and trim although they were dusty from the field.

Ben Thompson, though half a head taller, looked shrunken and miserable beside him. Cindy would have pitied Ben's shabbiness if she hadn't known he was the richest man in the county.

Cindy edged a little closer to her father, and he reached out and rumpled her hair with one hand. "Chores all done?" he asked.

"All done," she told him.

Ben Thompson peered at her from under his shaggy gray brows. "Ever put on a dress, young lady?" he demanded.

"Yes, sir. I wear dresses to school," she answered. She would have liked to remind him that he asked her the same question and got the same answer every time they met, but that wouldn't have been polite. She supposed he only asked the question because he couldn't think of anything else to say. Certainly he never listened to the answer. He just asked his question and then forgot about her, and went on talking to her father as if she didn't exist.

Ben stood leaning against Tom's manger, looking at the white horse and saying nothing for a long while. Watching him, Cindy wondered why he kept coming back, trying to buy the white team. Much as she loved them, she knew that they were nothing really special. They were just ordinary work horses, and middle-aged ones at that. Ben could have found any number of teams just as good, and bought them without argument for less than he had already offered her father. But it must be just as people said. Once Ben Thompson set his mind on something he wanted, he'd never give up until he got it. Old Ben, they said, could give a mule lessons in stubbornness.

Ben fixed his faded blue eyes on Tom and chewed the end of his ragged mustache. "Made up your mind to sell me that gelding, Dave?"

Cindy held her breath until her father shook his head. "Afraid I can't do that, Ben."

"Think not?" Ben drawled out the words, with a rusty chuckle at the end. "Well, suit yourself. Can't stand arguing with you all night. You think about it some more. How's the missus, Dave?"

Cindy's breath caught in her throat. People were always asking her father that question, and of course they meant well. But she wished they wouldn't. She stared hard at the layer of fine chaff on the floor, and stirred it with one toe while she waited for her father to answer. She breathed more easily when she heard his voice level and untroubled, just as it had been before.

"Coming along fine," he said.

"That so? Glad to hear it. When's she coming home?"

Cindy stole a look at her father, and saw the muscles along his jaw swell with tension. A vein at the side of his neck was throbbing hard and quick. But he waited scarcely longer than usual to answer, and his voice was slow and easy.

"Can't say for sure. Soon as she's able, I guess."

Ben said nothing. He looked at Dave Martin for a long moment from under his shaggy eyebrows, then for a shorter moment at Cindy. At last he turned and walked away.

Cindy glared after the old man. "Wouldn't hurt him to say good-bye," she muttered indignantly.

For a moment she thought her father wasn't going to answer. But then he said, "Can't remember when he ever did. Guess he figures hellos and good-byes are a waste of time. When Ben talks, he wants to make every word pay."

As she helped her father get Captain and Jerry cleaned up and ready to turn out to pasture, Cindy puzzled over what her father had just said. Old Ben was stingy and rude enough, but surely he wasn't quite that bad. After all, he'd joked with her about wearing a dress. He'd inquired about her mother. That meant he'd been willing to waste some words for politeness.

But—no, it didn't! Suddenly Cindy realized that what Ben had meant was more than what he had said. He'd been telling her father he had no right to turn down money he needed to buy dresses for his daughter, maybe even to make it possible for his wife to come home sooner.

Fired with anger at Ben's duplicity, Cindy curried Jerry with such energy that he winced away, with a little squeal of protest.

At last chores were finished for the night. Cindy went to let the cows out of their stanchions. When she came back, all the horses except Tom and Sade were already gone, and on their way down the lane to the pasture. She slipped off Tom's halter, and gave him a final pat as he backed out of his stall. Then she removed Sade's, and ran to join her father where he stood beside the watering trough. The sun was low, and the shadows of the orchard fell across the lane so that the cows and horses halfway down it seemed to fade out of sight. But because her team was white, she would be able to watch it all the way to the place where the lane curved around the corner of the orchard.

Tom had just come out of the barn. He tossed his head, and did a sort of gay, dancing step with an upward flick of his heels at the end of it. Then he turned back and stood still beside the barn door.

After a moment Sade appeared in the doorway. She walked with slow, hesitant steps, and at the doorway she stopped. For a moment she stood trembling, snorting softly with fear while she stretched her head through the doorway. Tom stepped closer, so that Sade's nose touched his side. Then she stepped over the doorsill and out into the barnyard.

Tom moved slowly toward the watering trough. Sade followed, and now she moved easily, with a steady, plodding step. They stopped and stood side by side to drink. Beside Tom's slender grace, Sade was heavy and lumpish. Her hoofs were twice the size of Tom's, her coat coarse and dull although it got the same careful grooming as Tom's. Cindy shook her head, thinking how lucky Sade had been to be teamed with Tom. Surely nobody would want her, just for herself. Timid and helpless as she was, probably she couldn't even live without him.

Tom finished drinking first, and stood waiting, twitching one ear back and forth with the look of a bored child twiddling his thumbs. Then he spied the red calf standing near the fence and lunged at him threateningly

with teeth bared. The calf blinked unconcernedly as
Tom's teeth snapped together a fraction of an inch
from his skin, and then strolled calmly away. Cindy
giggled. Poor Tom! There was hardly a creature on the
farm that hadn't learned how empty his menacing ges-
tures were. It was too bad, because he got such fun
out of scaring any of them.

Finally Sade lifted her head and reached to touch
Tom's side with her nose. Together, they turned away
and walked slowly down the lane. Long as she had
known them, often as she had watched them, Cindy still
looked with wide-eyed wonder. To her it was always a
marvelous thing to see how restless, lively Tom slowed
his steps to suit Sade's. Letting her pink nose rest gently
on his flank, he lifted his feet with exaggerated care at
any roughness in the ground. At the curve in the lane,
he swung wide and slow, so that she followed well clear
of any obstacle.

Cindy remembered something she had seen in a newspaper, about dogs that had been trained to guide blinded
war veterans. It took long and careful work to teach the
dog to lead and the man to follow. But here was Tom,
who did the same for Sade!

Only Tom had never been trained to lead, or Sade
to follow. Cindy's father had told her that. Tom and
Sade had been foaled a few weeks apart, the spring
when Cindy was four. When the white foals were
weaned, her father had turned them loose in the woods
pasture, where they could graze as they pleased and
drink from the stream. For months on end he'd hardly
seen them, and when now and then he did, it was hur-

riedly and without particular attention. He'd been too busy, most of the time, to remember them, because that had been 1917, the year the country had gone into the big war in Europe. Farmers were being urged to raise enough to feed the world, while at the same time the men they had been accustomed to hire to help them had disappeared into the army or into the factories. Of course Cindy couldn't really remember any of that, but she had heard it talked about so much that she was sure she knew how it had been.

Anyway, when at last her father had had time to notice the foals, it had already happened. Sade had gone blind, and Tom had become her guide. Somehow he had realized her need and learned how to meet it. Somehow Sade had learned to follow, trusting Tom as completely as if he had been part of herself.

"He's like her own eyes, isn't he, Dad?" Cindy said softly. "To see everything for her. Her seeing eye."

Cindy's father gave a little start. He blinked as if he had been suddenly awakened, and Cindy knew that although he had been looking at Tom and Sade he hadn't been thinking about them.

"Seeing eye? Yes, that's a good name for old Tom," he agreed. "Now, let's go get supper. It's late."

3 : A Lonesome House

Cindy shivered as she stepped into the chilly dampness of the old house. Once it had given her a fine, comfortable feeling to come through this door. There had been warmth here then, and voices, dishes rattling, the fire purring and crackling in the stove.

Now there was only the creaking of the door as her father opened it, the echo of their own footsteps, and the ticking of the clock. There was only a faint odor of kerosene, mingled with the musty, mildewed smell of old bricks and plaster. The air had the dead stillness of air unstirred by human movement. It sounded and smelled and felt like a place of dreadful emptiness, even after her father had lit the lamp, and the yellow rays had filled all the room except the shadowy corners.

But there was no look of emptiness. Except for a bit more dust and clutter, the kitchen looked the same as it always had. There was the big black cookstove at the end of the room. There was the tall kitchen cabinet, the big cupboards, the oilcloth-covered table and the chairs, the iron sink, the closed sewing machine covered with untidy stacks of magazines and books, the heavy walnut sideboard. There was the round-faced alarm clock, with its hands pointing to seven. There was the calendar with its straw-hatted, freckle-faced boy grinning at her above the page headed, SEPTEMBER, 1927. The shabby cluster of caps and jackets hanging on their row of pegs in the corner next to the stove, with the same dusty overshoes sprawled on the floor beneath them.

Dave Martin rubbed his hands together and gave himself a little shake. "Got to get a fire going here," he said. "About starved, Cindy?"

Cindy shook her head. "I fixed myself some bread and sugar when I came home. Had a couple of apples, too."

Quickly Dave began to make a fire. Lifting off one of the round black stove lids, he put in a crumpled sheet of newspaper. He added a handful of dry corncobs, and then a few sticks of wood. There were several corncobs standing on end in an open can of kerosene in the corner. He took one out, lit a match from a tin box hanging on the wall, and touched it to the kerosene-soaked cob. Then he thrust the blazing cob into the stove and dropped the lid into place. In a moment a fire was crackling, the smoke roaring up the chimney.

Meanwhile, Cindy dipped a washpan of water from the reservoir at the side of the stove, and carried it to the sink. The water held only a faint trace of warmth. Cindy watched her father as he tried to work up a lather on his hands.

"I could have started the fire," she said. "Water would have been warm by now."

Her father shook his head. "I start the fires around here. You know I always did, even for your mother."

Cindy didn't argue, although she thought her father

was being absurdly cautious. Then she remembered
the stark chimneys and the blackened remains of walls
she'd driven by with her father. Every time it had been
the same story. Someone, using kerosene to start a fire,
had used too much, or used it the wrong way.

"I could get the supper," Cindy suggested.

Her father shook his head. "You do enough. Just set
the table, and then rest a while. You look tired, Cindy."

"I guess I am, sort of." She took plates out of the cupboard and put them on the table, while her father started
supper.

He cut thick slices of ham, dropped them into a big
iron frying pan and set the pan on the stove. Then he
sliced cold boiled potatoes, dumped them into the other
side of the same pan, and sprinkled them generously
with salt and pepper. He opened a tin of peas into a
saucepan and shoved the pan onto the stove.

Only when these things were done did he pause to
look around. His eyes went to the sideboard, and then
to Cindy where she was getting knives and forks out of
a drawer in the cabinet.

"You looked for the mail?" he asked. He was trying
to sound as if he didn't really care.

Cindy said, "There wasn't anything. And I know the
carrier came, because I saw Mag Keller get mail out
of their box." One day she hadn't been sure, and Dad
had walked the long half mile to the mailbox and back
in a driving rain, just on the chance that a letter from
her mother was waiting there.

Cindy got water from the reservoir—it was warmer
now—and washed her face and hands. Then she sat

down at the table to wait. Hunger was gnawing at her stomach, but tiredness was hurting her all over. Now that there was nothing for her to do, she had time to feel it. The warmth from the stove crept through her like a drug. Her eyelids drooped. Her head sagged toward her plate.

Just in time Cindy caught herself, and shook herself sternly awake. She propped her elbows on the cold oil-cloth, and found the freckle-faced boy on the calendar staring at her. She hated that calendar. She couldn't sit down to a meal without seeing it, and being reminded of how long it had been since this kitchen had been a fine, warm place to come into.

There had been a dimpled, yellow-haired girl on the calendar then. The page had been headed NOVEMBER, 1926. It was Thanksgiving, that last day. Cindy remembered the wonderful last moment of that day. The peak of perfection, just before everything fell apart.

She remembered the big table in the dining room, spread with a linen cloth. There were two roast chickens on the table, big bowls of mashed potatoes, creamed onions, buttered beets, all steaming hot and giving out irresistible smells. There were bowls of cranberry sauce, plates of rolls, little dishes of homemade pickles and preserves, small platters of celery and olives and crisp strips of carrot.

Cindy was standing beside her chair, dressed in her best. She had on her black-and-white-checked taffeta with the lace collar, a new pair of white stockings, and patent-leather sandals. There was a big bow of red ribbon in her hair, a huge butterfly bow, the kind all the girls at school were wearing. She felt very elegant.

Dad was standing at the head of the table, wearing a white shirt and a necktie, and with his hair slicked down and shiny. Next to him came Marcy, looking angelic with her fair curls and her wide blue eyes. Then Grandpa Ellsworth, solid and dignified, with a dark-blue suit and a heavy gold watch chain. Grandma was at the foot of the table. She had bluish-white hair above a thin face, and always smelled of lilac perfume. Then there was little Davy, scowling fiercely because he had been made to sit in a high chair.

That was all of them except her mother. She had gone to the kitchen to fetch the gravy, which was kept simmering until the last moment on the back of the stove.

Cindy watched her mother through the kitchen door. Though she could see only one hand and a bit of her dark hair, she was picturing to herself how pretty her mother looked. She was very thin and straight, exactly like the pictures in the fashion magazines. Her hair was cut short, and curled by itself into glossy little swirls. She had cut it herself, the day before, snipping away with a big pair of scissors between glances first at the mirror that hung over the sink, then at the daring new style she had found in the new *Pictorial Review*. Her shining dark eyes looked too big for her thin face, and her cheeks were a bright glow of red.

Nobody in the world would have taken her mother for a farm wife, Cindy thought proudly. Nobody would have taken her for a mother of three children. She was so slim and pretty, so up to date with her short hair and her short skirts, the quick, restless way she moved and talked and laughed.

It was while Cindy was thinking all this that things began to happen. They happened so fast that she had never yet been able to straighten them out in her mind. There was a sudden crash and a thud from the kitchen. Then a time of fear and utter confusion.

Cindy remembered her father carrying her mother in his arms. She looked limp as a rag doll. Her father's face looked so angry that a stranger would have thought he was blaming her mother for falling. But Cindy knew that was the way he always looked when he was worried or afraid.

Marcy and Davy began to wail like scared babies. Grandma said in a shrill voice, "She's fainted!"

Grandpa roared, "Hush, all of you!" and in the sudden silence went over to take a closer look. Then he said in a strange, breathless voice, "She hasn't just fainted. She's really ill. Dave, we've got to get her to a doctor. We'll take her into town in my car. It'll be quicker than phoning him to come out. Better bring the little ones along, too. But hurry!"

That had seemed to last for a long time, but it couldn't have. For after Cindy had watched Grandpa's big Packard drive away down the dusty, rutted road and walked slowly back into the house, the food on the table was still warm.

It had been the most awful moment of Cindy's life when she had put her foot on the running board of Grandpa's car and Dad had frowned and motioned her away. Everyone else was in the car. Dad was sitting in the back seat, still holding her mother in his arms. Grandma was beside him, holding one of Mama's hands and looking frightened. Marcy and Davy were in the front with Grandpa. Cindy belonged there too, with her family.

But Dad said brusquely, "You'd better stay here, Cindy."

She stepped back, frightened and hurt. Everyone was going, and they didn't want her.

But then Dad said, "I don't know when we'll be back, Cindy. And somebody's got to be here to take care of the chores."

Back in the house, she fixed herself a plate piled high with Thanksgiving food. She was hungry, but after a few bites she found that she couldn't swallow any more.

Doing the chores all by herself that night made Cindy feel proud and important. But when the outside work was done, she had come in to see the table still set, the food uneaten. For a moment she had stood looking at the cold and crusted mashed potatoes, the onions congealed in their cream sauce, all the withered and discouraged things that a few hours ago had been so tempting. They were as ruined as the day.

She stepped through the kitchen door and then stopped short. Her eyes and mouth grew round with shock. The floor in front of the stove, the stove itself, even the nearby walls, were spattered and streaked with gravy. And scattered almost as widely were broken pieces of the dish her mother had been about to carry to the table. Mama's gravy boat, part of the lovely set of china that had been a wedding present, that she had prized so much she had never let Cindy, or even Dad, help set the table or dry the dishes when she used them! More than anything else, the sight of that broken dish made her realize how helpless her mother must have been before whatever it was that had struck her down.

Then Cindy turned and ran away. Upstairs, in bed with all her clothes still on, she cried herself to sleep.

Next morning she came down to find her father alone, looking pale and tired. Everything was in order, the ruined food gone, the dishes washed and put away. He must have worked hard, maybe all night, she thought.

He told her that they would have to look after things by themselves for a while. Her mother would have to stay in a hospital where she could rest and be looked after properly, and until she could come home Marcy and Davy would stay at Grandpa's house.

Cindy came back to reality with a start. Dad was scooping ham and fried potatoes onto her plate, right out of the frying pan. Before last Thanksgiving, food had always been served up properly, put into bowls and passed around.

Cindy sighed, and began to eat.

4 : Time for Fun

Cindy ate with determination but without enjoyment. The potatoes were burned at the edges, and soggy with grease. The ham was fried hard, and so salty she had to gulp milk quickly to wash away the taste. The factory-canned peas were pale and tasteless. Sometimes when Dad's cooking was particularly awful she managed to fill up with bread and butter. But tonight there wasn't any bread. The bakery man delivered twice a week, on Tuesdays and Saturdays, and what was left of Tuesday's bread had turned mouldy and had to be thrown away.

Out of the corner of her eye, Cindy stole a glance at her father. If he were staring into space with his thoughts miles away, she might be able to scrape her plate quickly into the garbage pail without his noticing how little she had eaten. But his eyes were on her, and his face looked worried. He was very strict about her eating everything that was on her plate.

Shoving another bite of potatoes into her mouth, she tried to imagine them tender and crisp and delicious, the way they had been when her mother was here to cook them. It didn't work.

Her father said anxiously, "What's the matter, Cindy?"

She swallowed hard and then took a sip of milk. "Those boughten peas are awful." She was ashamed to complain about anything Dad had cooked, when he tried so hard.

"You'd better get used to them," he growled. "We'll be eating them from now on."

Blinking back tears, she forced down another bite. Dad was right. She would get used to them, just as she had to the bakery bread. It had seemed soft and tasteless when they'd started using it just after her mother went away. But now she liked it fine.

Dad had explained why they had to learn to like the bakery bread and the factory-canned peas and all the other strange things, not just think of them as something to put up with until her mother came home. One of the things that had made her mother ill was too much hard work. When she came home again everything was going to be different. There would be no more baking, no more canning, no more running out to feed chickens or milk cows, no more sitting up late at night to sew and mend. Her mother would live like a town lady, the way she had been brought up to live.

The last bite was down, and Cindy sighed with relief. She didn't mind having no dessert. She was used to it now. Dad said sweet stuff cost too much, and besides you didn't need it if you ate a decent meal.

Cindy's father washed the day's dishes while she dried. There weren't many, for only two of them, but they were hard to wash. Egg had dried on the breakfast plates, and a coating of oatmeal had hardened inside a saucepan. Dad scowled with disgust as he scrubbed and scraped, and Cindy spent most of her time waiting for the next dish. That gave her time to think, and to remember Tom and Sade.

She was sure now that her father had thought about changing his mind. For a moment, money had meant more to him than her team. They did need money, she knew. But there must be some other way of getting it.

"Dad!" she cried eagerly. "Why can't you sell Jerry and Captain? They must be worth more than Tom and Sade. They're younger and stronger. And they're both sound."

Her father looked up from the dishpan. For a moment he seemed puzzled. "Oh! You're worried about your team? You heard me turn Ben down, didn't you?"

"But—" Cindy hesitated. "You were thinking about it. So you figured we could spare a team."

"Yes, we could spare one. But there's no market for work horses these days. You must have noticed yourself, everybody's getting tractors. Once a farmer's got one, he's trying to sell the horses he has, not buy more."

"Then why does Mr. Thompson want a work team?"

Her father shook his head. "Ben doesn't want just a work team. He wants this one. Like the time years ago he wanted a Cadillac. Paid a fancy price for it, too. Then he decided it cost too much to keep it in gas, so it's been sitting in his barn ever since. He didn't want that car to use. Just wanted it to have. Same way with this team. He doesn't need it. Just wants to have it. Maybe because he knows I don't want to sell."

"But that doesn't make sense!" Cindy cried.

"Guess it makes sense to Ben," her father said. "He spent his life making money and saving every penny he could. Did without most of the things people usually want to make their lives pleasant and comfortable, just so he could pile up more and more money. He's made money the most important thing in his life, and I guess he can't stand the idea that a couple of horses could mean more to anybody than the money he's willing to pay for them."

Cindy frowned, polishing a spoon. Then she looked up, and her face glowed with a sudden smile. "I'm glad we don't think that way."

Her father didn't return her look. His lips tightened, and when he finally spoke his voice was harsh. "Sometimes it's hard not to. Money can be pretty important when you don't have it." He scrubbed hard at the frying pan for what seemed a long time.

There was a knock at the screen door. Looking into the shadows outside, Cindy could make out only a tall shape, topped by a whitish blur. Ben Thompson! she thought despairingly. He must have come back, maybe to raise his price a few more dollars. In her father's present mood, discouraged and with the need for money so much on his mind, he might very well say yes. She dashed to the door with the wild hope of somehow getting rid of him before he had a chance to speak to her father.

"Oh!" Her gasp of surprise was half relief that it wasn't Ben, half pleasure at who it was. "Hi, Ted."

Seeing him, tall and lanky, with his thin face topped by hair bleached nearly white by the sun, she wondered

how even in the dim light she could have mistaken him
for Ben Thompson. Ted Nichols, who lived just down
the road in the house beside the bridge, was her oldest
friend. One of the first things she could remember was
the make-believe farm they had made in the yard,
the summer before Ted had started to school. And
summer after summer they had spent much of their
time together, running, climbing, swimming in the
creek, collecting insects—all sorts of fun. This summer
she had scarcely seen Ted. She had been too busy
even to think of fun. But seeing him now made her realize how much she had missed him.

Cindy's father crossed the room toward them, drying
his hands as he came. "Ted, how are you?"

"Fine, Mr. Martin. Could Cindy come for a swim?"

"Pretty late, isn't it? It's nearly dark."

Ted smiled with a gleam of white teeth. "We wouldn't
stay long. Frank's coming, and the Keller girls. And
I'd see Cindy got home all right."

"Please, Dad?" Cindy coaxed.

"All right. Just so you don't stay too late."

Cindy rushed upstairs to change into her bathing
suit. It was red wool, a little stiff and scratchy when it
was dry. Also, a little tight because she was growing so
fast now. Over it she put on one of her father's old
shirts, which reached almost to her knees, and hoped
he would consider her sufficiently dressed. He would
never allow her to go from her house to the swimming
hole in just her bathing suit, even though the way was
through the fields and no one but Ted would see
her.

They ran through a cornfield, across a pasture and a narrow lane and through another cornfield, with fences to be climbed between each one. Then they came to the steep bank that marked the edge of the creek. Climbing the levee, they made their way through a tangle of bushes and trees, and at the top looked down into darkness, shadowed by the levees and by tall trees whose branches met overhead. From below Cindy could hear laughter, and the sound of splashing.

Ted had been leading the way, a few yards ahead of her. Now he stopped, turned back, and reached for her hand. "Just hang onto me, Cindy."

Cindy jerked away. "Don't worry. I know the way." Ted needn't think he could treat her like a baby just because he was a little older.

Ted did not reply. He went on down the path, moving slowly just ahead of her. Cindy found that she didn't re-member the path as well as she had thought. During the summer, when she had been too busy to come here, tall weeds and bushes had grown into different shapes. The familiar bumps and holes in the path had been worn away and changed. Once she slipped at an unexpected turn, and Ted caught her arm and steadied her, then quickly let go. In a moment they were at the water's edge.

It was a little lighter there, or else Cindy's eyes had adjusted themselves to the darkness. She could see Ted's big brother Frank pulling himself up onto the bank, and the two Keller girls, Mag and Irene, standing in knee-deep water.

"Hi, Cindy!" they called, when they saw her. "Where

have you been all summer? Come on in! The water's warm as anything."

The water of the creek was still and greenish black. There was a narrow strip of pebbly sand on one bank, and on the higher bank opposite there was a diving board. Years ago Ted's father had fixed up the swimming hole, clearing the little beach and hauling gravel and sand for it, removing stumps and roots and big rocks that might endanger swimmers, putting up the diving board. Although it was on Nichols' land, neighbors were always welcome to use it. Cindy had been here often, in the summers before, but this year there hadn't been time. She had almost forgotten how nice it was.

Cindy slipped out of her shirt and sneakers and waded in. The water was hardly cooler than the air, but it felt delightful. It washed away the sweat and dust, the bits of straw and chaff from the barn, and made her skin feel smooth and new. She swam across the creek, dog paddle. Then she remembered that last summer Ted had started to teach her the Australian crawl. He said that was the stroke all real swimmers used. She started back determinedly, leveling out her body and kicking fast, the way he had showed her.

After a while she stopped, out of breath, and stood up in shoulder-deep water. Brushing back her wet hair, she looked around. Frank Nichols and the two girls were at the other end of the swimming area. Ted was nowhere in sight. She looked all around, scanning the banks, the shadowed darkness between the trees. Where could he have gone?

She remembered the way she had snapped at him when he had offered to help her down the bank. She had jerked her hand away as if she couldn't bear to touch him. And then, only a minute later, she had needed a helping hand. Then she'd been sorry, but hadn't known how to say so. Now Ted was probably mad at her, and she didn't blame him. After he'd been nice enough to come to the house and invite her, too!

Something caught her ankle and dragged her feet from under her. She sprawled into the water, then struggled up gasping and sputtering. "Ted, you—"

He was laughing at her. She flung herself at him, trying to duck him under. But he was too strong. Still laughing, he held her at arms' length while she wore herself out, and finally she began to laugh, too.

"I give up!" she panted. "When did you get so strong? A couple of years ago I could beat you, easy."

He grinned. "That was a couple of years ago. Bet you never will again. But you're strong, for a girl. Come on, let's sit on the bank a while and get our breath back."

They climbed up onto the grassy bank beside the diving board. Cindy draped her father's shirt around herself, pulling it down as far over her legs as it would go to keep off the mosquitoes.

After a moment Ted said, "I've missed you this summer, Cindy. I'll bet I've stopped by your house a dozen times, but you're never there. Then I've seen you out in one of the fields, cultivating or pitching hay, or something. Doing men's jobs, things my father won't even let me do yet. Why does your father make you do them?"

"He doesn't make me," Cindy told him indignantly. "It's just that there's so much work to do, and only him and me to do it. He used to hire a man to help, but since Mama's been sick he can't afford to pay one. So I help. You would, too, wouldn't you?"

"Well—sure I would," Ted agreed. "Sometimes I even wish Frank and Bob and Jim weren't around all the time. Then my father would need me to help, and I'd get a chance to try what I could do. But I still wouldn't want to have to work like you do, every day and all day. Everybody needs to have some time off for fun. But maybe things will change at your place pretty soon. Your mother's getting better, isn't she?"

Cindy sighed. "They keep saying she is. But they won't let me see her. And nobody knows when she'll be able to come home. Sometimes I think she never will, it's been so long."

"Oh, Cindy! Of course she will. You know this sickness she's got takes a long time to get over."

"Tuberculosis," Cindy said slowly. "Don't be afraid to say it. I'm not ashamed to admit that's what my mother has. No matter what some people are stupid enough to think."

"Now, why do you keep bringing that up all the time?" Ted demanded. "Sure, the kids were pretty mean to you when it first happened, but that was a long time ago. Why can't you forget it?"

Cindy set her chin stubbornly, and shook her head. "It's easy for you to talk. It didn't happen to you. First Mama went, and Marcy and Davy. Dad might almost as well have been gone, too. He acted so gloomy, and hardly spoke a word for days on end. That was the time my friends picked to let me down. They'd just sort of melt away in all directions when they saw me coming. If they were choosing up sides for a game, nobody took me. They just went ahead as if I weren't there. Nobody would even sit beside me on the bus. They'd stand up first. Think that was fun?"

"I know," Ted admitted. "It must have been awful."

"The worst thing was not knowing why," Cindy went on angrily. "Some nights I couldn't sleep, wondering what I could have done or said to get them all so mad at me. Or sometimes I'd stand in front of the mirror, just looking at myself. Trying to figure out why all of a sudden nobody could stand me, when they always seemed to like me before."

"Will you cut it out?" Ted demanded sharply. "It's all over. And it didn't last long. Miss Emery straightened things out as soon as she noticed what was going on, didn't she? Going over to high school, I never even heard anything about it until it was over."

Cindy smiled ruefully. "Miss Emery straightened out everybody but me, I guess. I couldn't imagine why she skipped over to the back of the hygiene book and took two whole periods talking about tuberculosis. How it was a serious illness, but nothing to get panicky about. How people caught it, how it was treated, how most people were cured if they got the right care in time. How careful the doctors were to make sure nobody else in the patient's family had it, or to get them cured if they did. That made them realize they'd been silly to be afraid of catching some deadly plague from me. But nobody told me what was wrong with Mama. Everybody else in town knew before she got settled in the hospital, but not me. It was a couple of days after those lectures before I remembered how Dad had taken me to Dr. Mason right after Mama went away, and the doctor went over me as if I'd been a horse he was getting ready to buy. Then I knew, and I went to Dad and asked him right out. And then he finally told me."

"Your Dad meant well," Ted said comfortingly. "He just didn't want to worry you."

"I don't blame him," Cindy said. "I can't even blame them, exactly. They'd heard so many scary things about it. But I can't help thinking, suppose they heard something else about me. Would they act the same way, without even asking if it was true, or if it was as bad as they thought?"

Ted looked at her and shook his head. "Honest, Cindy! Haven't you got enough trouble without bringing up what happened last year, and then borrowing what might never happen? Come on, now. Let's swim some more."

"Bet I can stay under water longer than you can." Cindy jumped from the board, down under the dark water, throwing her shirt to the ground as she went. Ted hit the water a second later. She made up her mind she wouldn't come up first. Nothing could make her. The seconds went by, slowly and more slowly. Her chest ached, and her head began to pound. At last she gave up. Ted emerged an instant later, and they declared the contest a tie. Also, it was quite dark. Time to be going home.

"It was fun, Ted," she told him at the door. "Sorry for crying all over your shoulder."

"That's all right," he told her. "Hope you feel better, getting that stuff off your chest."

She nodded. "I do. There hasn't been anybody to talk to for so long. I can't worry Dad with my troubles. He's got enough of his own."

"I guess so," Ted agreed. "See you again soon, hm?"

Cindy nodded. "I'm awfully glad you came. Good night."

Her father was sitting at the kitchen table. There was a magazine open in front of him, but he wasn't reading it. He was just staring, with a strange, angry expression, into the darkest of the shadowy corners. When the door opened he looked around.

"Guess I don't have to ask if you had a good time," he said. "Better get to bed now." He lighted her small lamp and handed it to her.

As she carried it through the dark hallway and up the stairs, Cindy moved in a wavering circle of yellowish light. Black shadows retreated ahead, and closed in behind her. The open doorway to her room looked like the entrance to a cave where any sinister thing might lie in wait.

5 : An Alarm in the Night

Cindy took a deep breath and stepped through the doorway. The blackness shrank into the corners of the big room, and there was nothing except the same old furniture. She set the lamp on the table by the head of her bed, undressed, and slipped into her flannel nightgown.

Once in bed, she propped herself up with her pillow and picked up *The Deerslayer* from the table. She had read it twice before, but it was still exciting. In less than a minute Cindy was picking her way stealthily through the forest, alert for any sign of a hostile redskin. And, at the same time, she was in her own bed, alert for the first sound of her father's footsteps on the stairs. He did not approve of her reading in bed, saying crossly that it wasted oil. Cindy suspected, however, that what he really worried about was her sleep, though he considered it unmanly to say so.

In the middle of a sentence she heard him coming and instantly put down the book and blew out the lamp. She wriggled about, trying to find a comfortable place in the lumpy bed. The mattress hadn't been emptied out and filled with fresh straw after threshing this year, as it would have been if her mother had been here. She must remember to turn it over tomorrow and shake it well.

The room felt lonesome. Cindy said her prayers in a

whisper, and for a moment felt better. But only for a moment. The trouble was that there was moonlight coming through the windows at the other end of the room. She could see the two small beds with their bare slats making black stripes on the floor. When she turned on her other side, it was even worse. She couldn't see the beds, but now she imagined them the way they used to be, with Marcy and Davy in them. They had always come upstairs together, her mother carrying Davy while Cindy held Marcy's hand. Always her mother had tucked each of them in and kissed them good night. Then, after she had gone downstairs, Cindy had told stories to the little ones until they went to sleep. The room had been a friendly place then. They had called it "The Three Bears' House," because of the three beds of different sizes. That had been the story Cindy had told oftenest, too. She had changed it about a good deal, putting in funny things when she thought of them, or sometimes scary things. But not too scary, because of Davy being so small. Thinking of Davy laughing with delight when she imitated the squeaky voice of the baby bear, Cindy burrowed her head into the pillow and held her breath until the shameful wish to cry went away.

Marcy and Davy probably wouldn't believe she missed them so much. Cindy remembered remorsefully how often she had told them they were pests and babies, how many times she had wished aloud that she had her own room where she could read in peace. Sometimes she'd said it just to make sure they knew how lucky they were to have a big sister who would put up with them.

But there were times when she had really meant it. She could never have imagined feeling this way because they were gone.

She wondered if Ted realized how lucky he was to have his mother and father and his three big brothers all sleeping safely in the house with him. But of course he didn't. People never knew how important their families were until somebody was gone. Then they found out. Maybe Ted would find out some day, too. But suddenly she found herself wishing very hard that he never would. Ted was so nice, so good-tempered, so sensible. He was the only one of the people she cared about who hadn't gone away from her, or changed.

Well, there was her team, too. Tom and Sade hadn't changed either. Of course they weren't people, but she had loved them so long they almost seemed to be. She thought about Sade depending on Tom, feeling safe and comfortable when he was around. Cindy had felt a bit the same about Ted tonight, she thought, as Sade must feel about Tom. Not that she was helpless like Sade, of course. But it was good to lean on someone who felt safe in the world, when you didn't.

Startled out of her sleep, Cindy sat straight up in bed. A terrible screeching and squawking seemed to be right in the room with her. In a moment she realized that it was coming from the henhouse. Something had scared the chickens into an uproar. Maybe a thief. Some of the neighbors had been losing poultry.

But chilly, pale-gray light was creeping through the window. It was beginning to be morning. A thief would come in darkness. It must be a fox or a weasel. But then why wasn't Shep chasing it away? He must be off hunting rabbits somewhere, Cindy supposed, just when he was needed.

Quickly she jumped out of bed and into her clothes. She hurried down the stairs and through the silent house. On her way down the path, she stooped to pick up a stick. Probably just the scent of her would be enough to frighten a fox away, but it would be good to have something in her hand.

The heavy dew on the grass and weeds was cold on her bare feet, and colder still where it had soaked through the legs of her overalls. Her teeth chattered, partly from the chill and partly from the fearful excitement of dashing headlong into unknown perils. Frightful squawks were coming from the henhouse, and as she came nearer two hens flapped wildly through a window and fled in the direction of the orchard.

Cindy tore around the corner of the building and skidded to a stop. Her mouth dropped open in astonishment. She had nearly run into a huge white shape that loomed ahead of her, ghostly in the dimness. It was a short but breathless moment before she recognized the shape as the rear part of Tom. His head and neck were inside the henhouse.

The thought of how astonished the hens must have been, waking from peaceful sleep to see Tom's big white head and neck protruding into their bedroom, made Cindy nearly collapse with laughter. But after a moment she managed to raise her stick and prod Tom sharply in the ribs.

Tom gave a startled backward leap. The flimsy structure creaked and swayed. Suddenly Tom's predicament stopped being funny.

"Whoa! Steady, Tom. Whoa, there." Cindy dropped the stick and sprang to the doorway, as near the horse's head as she could get. Her small hands stroked his shoulder reassuringly. Her voice was soothing. Tom must have lowered his head to get it through the door. He would have to lower it again to get it out, and he'd never do that while he was scared or excited. If she could only get inside, she could coax his head down and back him out. But there was no getting through the doorway, because that was completely filled by Tom.

"Oh!" she cried despairingly. "What am I going to do with you, you old stupid?"

There was a chuckle behind her. "No use calling him names, Cindy. He knows you think he's the smartest horse alive." When she looked around, her father was standing with his shotgun under his arm shaking with silent laughter.

Cindy giggled. "Well, he is smart. He loves eggs. Do you think he figured out this is where to find lots of them?"

Her father shook his head and laid the shotgun carefully down. "Horses don't think. It's just that Tom's always got to be poking his nose in where it doesn't belong. And it's up to us to get it out before he knocks down our henhouse. Just one way I can think of to do that. In you go, Cindy."

He gave her a boost through the narrow window space, and she dropped inside. The small building was dark, filled with the sound and smell of chickens. The air was heavy with dust, chaff, and a storm of tiny feathers. A squawking fowl dashed between Cindy's feet, and another plummeted against her chest. Fending off panicky hens with both hands, she sneezed hard three times. After a moment she could see a little.

Tom's big white head and part of his neck blocked the door. His ears were laid back, and the whites of his eyes were showing just a bit. He snorted nervously, blowing more dust and chaff into the air. Unless Cindy could calm him, panic might take over at any instant. Then he would struggle wildly for escape. The henhouse would be smashed, and Tom himself might be hurt.

Slowly, with infinite care, Cindy moved toward Tom. Very gently she talked to him, her voice never stopping for an instant. It didn't matter what she said. The important thing was the soothing, calming voice, telling Tom that she was here and that she wasn't afraid. Telling Tom that nothing could hurt him, now that Cindy was here.

Her small hand touched Tom's broad cheek, and then gripped the coarse long hair of his mane. The other hand scratched gently for a moment at Tom's forehead, then slid down his nose and rested firmly just above his nostrils.

"Back, Tom. That's it. Just a little more."

She could feel the tension in him, the desire to toss his head high, to strike out with his hoofs, to do anything to force his way out of this dark, smelly, noisy trap. But with a gently persistent pressure she eased him back through the doorway and followed into the delightful freshness of outdoors. Then she gave a great sigh of relief.

"Good work, Cindy! I knew you could do it." She and her father followed Tom as he ambled toward the barn. Now that it was over, he looked smug and self-satisfied, not in the least ashamed of all the trouble he had caused.

And now, of course, here came Shep, tearing along beside the pasture fence. As if to make up for his late arrival, he dashed close to Tom's heels, barking officiously. Tom squealed angrily, and lashed out with a hoof that ruffled the long hair on Shep's neck. Shep didn't even flinch. He knew the emptiness of Tom's threats better than anyone else. Not until Tom had passed through the half-open gate by the watering trough did he turn away, wagging his bushy tail as proudly as if he had done the job all by himself.

Dad frowned. "That Tom! The old rascal! Thank goodness none of the rest of the stock got out." Sade was standing patiently just inside, but none of the other animals was in sight.

Cindy waited while her father found a piece of baling wire and wired the gate closed. It was a good gate, with a fine patent latch. But the latch hadn't been invented that Tom couldn't figure out, once he took it into his head to try.

"Might as well put him to work, as long as he's feeling so frisky," Cindy's father decided. "We'll dig out a few potatoes before breakfast."

Cindy got the horses into the barn, and her father harnessed them. Tom stamped and snorted indignantly at finding no food in his manger, but Sade, patient as usual, only blinked her cloudy eyes and looked sad.

As they walked up the lane toward the potato patch, Cindy yawned and rubbed her eyes. But after a moment she decided it was good to be up and out so early. The air was fresh and clean, though a little chilly. The first rays of the sun struck the dewdrops that covered the tall grass and weeds along the edge of the lane, and made them glow and sparkle like jewels. Cindy and her father seemed to move through a sleeping world, where the creak of harness, the jingle of trace chains and the muffled clump of hoofs in the dust were the only sounds. Then a rooster crowed, and from far away a train whistled mournfully.

"I wish I knew how they talk to each other," Cindy said wistfully.

"Hm?" Her father looked down at her. "How who talks?"

"The horses. How did Sade know to stay there and wait for Tom? Of course I know they don't really talk, but he must tell her some way to wait for him. How do you suppose he does?"

"I guess the same way a mother animal tells her young ones not to move until she comes back."

Cindy frowned. "But that's instinct. They said so in school. Baby animals just know, and when they grow up they forget."

"Hm. That's right. Well, then, I suppose it's because they're a team. Sade just knows Tom will come back, because they belong together. There's something about a team, Cindy. You've watched horses enough to know. When they've been together for a while they're not just two horses any more. I don't mean only Tom and Sade. Take Jerry alone, and he can't pull anywhere near half the load he can when he's with Captain. Split up a good team that's been together a long time, and you've got two separate nothings."

Tom flung his head high, his ears alert. He snorted softly, and his trim black hoofs moved in a little dancing step. Sade plodded along, heavy-footed, her head low. Cindy sighed. "Tom's always leaving her, though, to have fun. Remember how he used to untie the halter rope with his teeth, and then unfasten the hook on the barn door and gallop wild all over the place?"

Her father nodded grimly. "It's a good thing we stopped that. Using a strap fastened with a buckle was a little too much, even for Tom."

Cindy giggled. "He'll think of something else to surprise us. Remember when he jumped the saggy place in the garden fence and ate all the lettuce? And the time he nibbled the hair off Marcy's doll, when she left it too close to the fence?"

"You're right, I do! When I think of the damage that old pest has done, I wonder why I didn't jump at a chance to sell him."

Hastily Cindy changed the subject. "I meant, Tom likes fun so much. And Sade never does anything. Maybe he doesn't like being a team with Sade. Maybe when he gets away he doesn't want to come back. Maybe he'd be glad if he didn't have to."

"Now, you know that's silly!" The look her father

gave her was so scornful, it was plain he didn't think she was worth talking to.

Cindy lagged behind, scuffing her feet in the dust. It seemed that lately she was always saying something wrong. She wished she could figure out what it had been this time.

6 : Saturday Scrubbing

Cindy watched her father hitch Tom and Sade to the potato digger and start off down the first row. As the horses leaned into the traces, hard ridges of muscle stood out under their smooth white coats. Her father clucked to them encouragingly. The blade pulled hard through the dry earth, bringing up the top layer of soil with the potatoes in it, carrying it back over an open-work conveyor that let the dirt fall through and dropped the potatoes off behind. The horses pulled at a slow, steady pace. Cindy trailed along, watching expectantly.

Just as she had known it would, it happened. Not all at once, but little by little, the tension of Tom's traces eased. Though he still held his head low and lifted his feet slowly as if he were pulling hard, the bulging muscles smoothed. Tom's long white tail swept sideways to brush a fly from his leg. Sade breathed hard, pulling with all her might. Her legs quivered, bracing them-selves at each step for the next tremendous effort. Cindy counted the steps before her father noticed, each one a triumph for Tom.

Even when he noticed, Dad didn't yell. He never yelled at horses, as some people did. His voice was stern, and just loud enough. "You—Tom!"

Even before the end of the rein flicked sharply against

his flank, Tom sprang forward. Cindy thought with delight that few people, and certainly no other horse, could have expressed so much injured innocence without making a sound.

She glanced up at her father. His lips were pressed tight together, but there was a glint of amusement in his eyes. Often as he got angry with Tom, he could never stay that way long.

Cindy took a half-bushel basket from beside the fence and started to pick up potatoes. Only the good smooth ones, bigger than an egg, went into the basket, for they were to be sold. The small ones, and the larger ones that had grown into strange, knobby shapes, would be gathered up later and used at home.

Bent double over the row, Cindy gathered up potatoes and put them into the basket, carefully so that they wouldn't be skinned or bruised. Though the machine was supposed to leave them neatly on the surface, it didn't always work that way. She had to sift through the dirt with her hands to make sure none had been buried, and found one often enough not to dare neglect the chore. A sharp stone cut into one finger. Cindy wiped the oozing blood on an old handkerchief she found crumpled in the bottom of one of her pockets, and then went ahead with her work. At school she could recite glibly the facts about germs, and tell how necessary it was to wash, disinfect and bandage even the tiniest scratch. But home was a different world, where hurts came too often and too inconveniently. They were simply ignored.

She worked automatically, filled one basket, fetched

another and filled that. Picking up potatoes was the worst job she could think of, but she wasn't sure why. Strawberries took as much bending, and melons were even heavier. But those things had delightful smells, and eating them was a special treat. Potatoes were necessary but dull—drab in color, earthy in smell, insipid in taste.

Luckily, her father had dug out only two rows. He left the horses standing, and came to help her finish. He worked fast, using a bushel basket, and in next to no time the rows were bare. He dumped the baskets into gunny sacks, and carried the sacks to the gate where he would pick them up later with the truck. Cindy trailed behind, watching him admiringly.

Not many men could balance a bushel on each shoulder and walk easily over rough ground. She had heard neighbors brag of their feats of strength—big, rough men who would make two of her father. Dad never joined in. He only smiled and kept silent, holding his own strength until he needed it, then using it quietly, as if it were nothing special. Her father was the most wonderful person in the world.

After the chores were done and they had eaten a quick breakfast it was time to settle down to what Cindy called their Saturday scubbing. This was the day they did housework—laundry, cleaning, shopping. The first job was washing clothes.

Cindy went through the rooms, gathering dirty clothes into a big basket. By the time she had finished, Dad had a fire going in the stove in the washhouse, and the boiler on top of it filled with water.

He started the noisy, one-cylinder gasoline engine that ran the washing machine. Then, with sleeves rolled high, he filled the big wooden tub with steaming water, dumped in a cake of laundry soap cut up into little chunks, and dropped in the white clothes. While they washed, he brought water for the rinsing tub, and mixed up a panful of starch.

The wringer had to be turned by hand, with a crank. Cindy watched the muscles in her father's arms bulge as he put the clothes through it, and for the first time wondered how her mother had managed the job. As she hung the clean things on the line, she resolved that this was one more thing Mama would never have to do again after she came home.

While the clothes were drying, Cindy and her father went to work on the house. They went through the bedrooms, the halls, and the kitchen, sweeping, scrubbing, dusting, putting things in order. They worked with brisk efficiency, and in silence. The sooner it was done, the sooner they could be out and away, doing the things they liked to do.

When they had finished, everything was neat and spotless, in order for another week. The house looked much tidier, Cindy thought, than it had ever looked when her mother was home. But then it had felt nice to come into. The house had welcomed you then, and made you want to stay. Now it was just a place to come when you had to, and to leave as soon as possible with a feeling of relief.

The rooms she and her father didn't need to use were shut up tight, their shades drawn and their furniture covered with old sheets or spread-out newspapers to keep off the dust. Cindy opened the parlor door a crack and peered inside. There, white-covered and ghostly, was the piano her mother used to play for them, in the evenings or on Sunday afternoons. There was the very bench where she used to sit, with the top that lifted up to disclose stacks of sheet music, all old, some nearly worn out from handling. There were hymns, old songs, waltzes, polkas, and Cindy's favorites, the gay ragtime melodies. When her mother played those, her slender fingers flew so fast they turned to a pale blur of movement.

This room had been empty, silent, untouched for almost a year. Dust lay thick on the sheeted furniture, and on the layers of newspaper that covered the carpet. Cobwebs clung in the corners, and along the edges of the drawn blinds. Still, this room seemed warmer and more alive than the ones she and her father used every day. Cindy swallowed hard, closed the door and turned away.

She and her father had a lunch of sandwiches and milk, and then her father went about his outside work. Cindy looked after him and envied his freedom. There was no escape for her yet, with the ironing still to be done.

The clothes had dried fast. Cindy took them down from the line, and while the three irons heated on the stove she folded the things that didn't need ironing. There wasn't really much that did. Only Dad's good shirt and her own dresses. Everyday things were only smoothed and worn rough dried.

Ironing was a tedious job, mostly because the irons cooled so fast. Every few minutes she had to put back the one she was using and get the hottest one from the stove. Still, it was fun to watch the dull, rough fabric turn smooth and shining under the iron, and to smell the clean, steamy ironing smell. She finished her father's white shirt and her old brown-and-white striped dress.

She shook out a blue-and-white gingham, and frowned with dismay. The seam under one arm had ripped a couple of inches yesterday morning when she was dressing for school. Being in a hurry, she had pinned it together with a safety pin and worn it anyway. Now the fabric had split crossways in both directions from the pin.

She took out the pin and carefully ironed the dress. Now the damage looked worse than ever. And it had been her best dress. Maybe she could fix it, she thought hopefully. She went to fetch her mother's sewing basket and scrap bag.

With relief she saw that there was a good-sized piece of material in the scrap bag, left over from when Mama had made the dress more than a year ago. It wouldn't really match now, because the dress had faded, but that couldn't be helped. Cindy set her jaw determinedly, and after some difficulty managed to thread a needle.

What in the world to do next? She glared at the dress for a moment in anger and despair. Then she grabbed the scissors, whacked off a big chunk of material, and began to sew it with big, hasty stitches to the outside of the dress. At last it was done. She held it up, and found that she had sewed right through the patch and both sides of the dress. A moment later the dress was a crumpled heap in the corner. Cindy put her head down on the table, biting her lips to keep from crying.

"Hey, Cindy! What happened? Why are you crying?"

"I'm not crying. Go away!" If anything could have made Cindy more miserable, it was to have Ted find her like this.

"Go away? Well, I like that. I just got here. I don't know what's bothering you, but don't bite my head off about it. It's not my fault. If you burned your hand ironing, maybe I can find you something to put on it."

"I didn't burn my hand." Cindy looked up to glare at Ted. But when she saw the worried look on his face, she couldn't help laughing. "I guess I'm just mad at myself for being so stupid." She picked up the dress to show him.

Ted grinned. "You sure messed that up," he agreed. "Don't you know how to sew at all?"

"Not a bit," Cindy admitted. "Mama was always going to teach me. But whenever she could spare a little time, I'd always be outside helping Dad with some of the chores."

"So you can't patch a dress, and what's the difference? You can do plenty of other things most kids can't do." Ted spread out the dress, looked at it and shook his head. "Looks like a pretty hard job. Better bring it over and let my mother show you how."

"Oh—I couldn't do that."

"Why not?" Ted demanded. "She'd like to. She was

saying just the other day she wished you'd come over and see us the way you used to. She worries about how you and your father get along, but—"

"I know." Cindy could feel her face getting red. Mrs. Nichols, like several other neighbor women, had come to the house after her mother had gone away, with offers of help. Her father had made it plain to them all that he neither needed nor wanted any. Without actually saying anything rude, he had sent each of them away offended and hurt, so that they had never come back. All her life before, Cindy had spent much time in the Nichols' house. But since then she had stayed away. Because Ted was as friendly as ever when they met, she had supposed he knew nothing about the way her father had acted. Now, his unfinished remark made her realize that he had known all along.

"Anyway, I couldn't go now," she said. "I have to go to town with Dad."

"I'll tell you what!" Quickly Ted rolled the dress around the piece of extra material and tucked it under his arm. "I'll take it home with me now, and ask Mom about it. You can come and get it when you have time. See you!"

"Stop!" Cindy wailed. But Ted was already halfway down the walk running fast, with her best dress under his arm.

7 : A Trip to Town

The old model-T truck jounced across the railroad tracks, past the grain elevator that towered like a giant above every other building in Walnut Grove. It passed a few scattered houses, and then the school. From her seat beside her father, Cindy looked out at the dingy brick building with the iron pump in front and the two red-painted wooden buildings in back.

"Just think," she told her father excitedly, "next year I'll be going way over to Centerville, to the high school. It's got bathrooms inside, and drinking fountains, and a gymnasium. Can you imagine it?"

Her father nodded. "Sure, I can. It's only right. All schools ought to be like that. Just you wait, Cindy. Before long we'll have those things at home, too. Bathroom and water, I mean. Don't suppose we need a gymnasium."

Cindy giggled. "I guess we can get along without that. Just so we get the rest."

"Would you like a pink bathtub, Cindy? They're the newest thing."

"Oh—I don't know." Cindy turned away and stared out the window, frowning. Her father sighed and said no more.

She knew she should have gone on, talking and letting

her father talk, about the pink bathtub, and the lino-
leum on the floor, and the curtains at the windows. But
she couldn't. It was silly to talk about it. None of it was
going to happen.

Good things used to happen, before her mother went
away. There had been the sink in the kitchen, which
let water drain outside instead of being carried out.
There was no water running in, because that would
have cost too much. There had been the pure-bred
Jersey bull, bought as the foundation of a fine dairy
herd. There had been the car, shiny and almost new,
to replace their rattly old one.

But since last Thanksgiving, everything had been slipping away. First the car. Then the dairy herd, except
for the two least valuable cows. If it had been worth
anyone's while to carry it away, Cindy thought gloom-
ily, the kitchen sink would have been gone, too.

It was hard to understand how things had slid down-
hill so fast. It wasn't just that paying the hospital and
the doctors had drained away lots of money. Besides
that, the money hadn't been coming in the way it usually did. Dad worked as hard as he could, from morning till night. Cindy worked as hard as she could to
help. But nothing ever seemed to turn out right.

It didn't seem as if her mother's being away should
make so much difference. She had never lent a hand
in the field at haying time or corn husking, as most of
the neighbors' wives did. She was so slim and frail, and
even after all the years on the farm still so frightened
of animals and bugs, that Dad had never let her do
even such little things as bring him lunch and a fresh

team at noon. She didn't even drive a car, so that she could save Dad time by running errands for him, or fetching things from town. Even such ordinary women's work as milking cows or feeding chickens, she did only now and then, when Dad was simply too busy to find time for them. Cindy really couldn't see why things should have started going wrong as soon as she left. But they had.

So maybe when her mother came home things would change, and good things would begin to happen again. But until then it was no use even thinking about them.

Walnut Grove was a pretty town, with brick-paved streets lined with tall shade trees. Its houses were neat, with well-kept yards and neat vegetable gardens.

They passed a large, dingy building in which farm implements were sold and repaired. Until a few years ago it had been a livery stable, and horses had been kept in it.

Cindy's father drove the truck up to the loading platform of the creamery, and a scrawny, red-haired man who had been sweeping it with a push broom picked up a couple of empty cans and brought them over.

"Stay where you are, Dave," he called, "I'll get it." He reached into the back of the truck and lifted out the two cream cans. "Got your check inside. Come on, Cindy. You get it. Save your old Daddy and me a few steps."

Cindy scrambled out, and followed him through the heavy door into a coldness that for a moment made her catch her breath. Then she blew out gently, with her mouth open, to watch the cloud of whiteness it made in the air. She had stepped into winter, all in an instant.

The red-haired man smiled, and thrust two fingers into the breast pocket of his white overalls. "Had it here all the time," he said in a conspirator's voice. "Figured you'd like a chance to cool off. Help yourself to ice." He waved invitingly at a case where chips of ice were packed around bottles of milk.

"Thank you," said Cindy. She took the check carefully in one hand, and dipped greedily for ice with the other. Then she ducked quickly through the door the creamery man was holding open for her, and scrambled back into the truck.

With her mouth full of ice that made her teeth ache with cold and yet was delicious, Cindy scrubbed her dripping right hand on her overalls and forgot to look out the window until they were almost past the pool room. But she remembered just in time, and watched it closely until it was out of sight. She always did that, hoping sometime to see something happen that would explain its vaguely evil reputation. But nothing did.

By the time Cindy took her fascinated eyes from the pool room, they had driven by the bright new chain grocery store which had opened the month before, the barber shop, and the hardware. They stopped in front of Schwartz's. Dad lifted the crate of eggs out of the back of the truck. Cindy ran to hold the door open for him, then followed him inside.

Schwartz's Grocery and Dry Goods was dark and cool, like a cave. Not a scary cave, but a cozy one that smelled of cheese and bacon, coffee, tobacco, and leather. It took a few minutes before her eyes adjusted themselves to the dimness and she could see Mr. Schwartz, tall, pale and spindly like a plant that has sprouted in a dark place. He stood behind the grocery counter, in front of rows of bins neatly labeled FLOUR, RICE, WHITE SUGAR, and so on. Above them a row of glass canisters held the staples sold in smaller quantities, such as pepper and cocoa. A glass case displayed cheese and a variety of smoked meats, lard, peanut butter, dill pickles. Farther along were shelves of canned goods, and finally the barrels that held vinegar and molasses. Across the narrow end were household necessities —brooms, mops and soap. Then, around the corner and along the other wall, was the dry goods department. Shelves were stacked with bolts of cloth, boxes of shirts, underwear, shoes, socks. Near the front another glass case, this one filled with tobacco, pencils, shoe laces, thread, and all sorts of small articles, and on top glass jars of licorice whips, peppermint drops, horehound sticks, and jelly beans. A stalk of bananas hung from the ceiling, and under it stood two wooden boxes which sometimes held oranges and lemons.

Whenever Cindy came into Schwartz's she looked to see whether there were any oranges and lemons. That was the only thing that ever changed. Today there were no oranges, and barely enough lemons to cover the bottom of the box.

Mr. Schwartz moved nimbly about behind the counter, scooping rolled oats from a bin with one hand while he flicked open a paper bag and set it on the scales with the other, folding over the top of the filled bag while he reached for string, wrapping the string around, tying the knot and snapping off the string, all faster than Cindy's eyes could move to watch.

Cindy concentrated on the things she wished her father would ask for—peanut butter, cocoa, bananas. She wouldn't ask, but maybe if she thought about them hard enough the idea of buying them would fly into his mind.

It didn't work. She hadn't really expected it to. Only the dullest necessities—vinegar and salt and laundry soap—were on the counter with the oatmeal when her father said, "I guess that'll be all."

Mr. Schwartz punched a button on the cash register, the little drawer flew open, and he took out some change and dropped it into Dave Martin's hand. "You came out a little ahead, Dave. Even with eggs down a penny a dozen."

They stopped next at the bank. Cindy sat on a bench in the lobby, while her father went straight back to the office. There was nothing to do while she waited. No magazines to look at, as in a doctor's or dentist's office. Nothing but a wispy-looking man in a green eyeshade standing in a cage and counting money. It was a terrible lot of money, but not interesting because none of it was hers.

In a moment her father and Mr. Sands, the president of the bank, came out of the office. Mr. Sands was shaking his head. "That cream check pays your overdue interest, and I've extended your notes another thirty days. But how long can you go on spending more than you make? You've put up a good fight, Dave, but I don't know how you can hold out much longer."

On the way home, Cindy sat silent. When she glanced at her father his face looked old. Deep lines showed between his eyebrows, and his mouth was thin and tight. She was glad when they approached the Nichols' place, and she could say, "I'd like to get off here, please. Got to see Mrs. Nichols about something."

Her father looked surprised, but he didn't ask any questions. Just stopped the truck and let her out, then went on down the road toward home.

Cindy walked slowly up the drive, wishing Ted were in sight. But there didn't seem to be anyone around. The Franklin touring car and the Chevrolet truck were not in their usual parking places in the turnaround between the house and the barn. Everything was very quiet. Maybe they were all gone, Cindy thought hopefully. Maybe Mrs. Nichols had mended her dress and left it on the long porch at the side of the house. That would be perfect. Or maybe she had refused to mend it, saying that people who were too proud to take favors had no business to ask for them. Well, that was all right too. If she found the dress unmended on the porch, that was what it would mean. She would be ashamed, but not so much as if she had had to face Mrs. Nichols and hear her say it.

The Nichols' house was older than the one where Cindy lived. It was lower and plainer, and its brick was covered with cream-colored paint that was peeling off in spots. But it looked comfortable and cared for. Asters and marigolds bloomed along the picket fence that enclosed the dooryard. The brick walk that led up to the side door was shaded by an arbor covered with grape vines. There were no grapes left now, and the leaves were curling and ready to drop. Cindy could hardly believe that only the summer before last she and Ted had spent long afternoons lounging in the shade of the arbor, idly eating the purple grapes, the big, tart pale-green ones, and the little, sweet pink ones. They had talked about everything that came into their heads, played guessing games, argued, teased each other. They had often been bored, and complained to each other of having nothing to do. For a moment Cindy wished she'd known how soon that idle, placid time would end, so that she could have appreciated it. Then she was glad she hadn't.

Cindy peered through the screen at the long porch with its shabby, comfortable furniture. It was empty. No sign of her blue-and-white-gingham dress. She knocked timidly, and waited. No one came. Softly she opened the screen door and walked across the porch to the open kitchen door.

The very sight and smell of Mrs. Nichols' kitchen made Cindy wince at a quick stab of mingled hunger and lonesomeness. So many times she and Ted had run through this door, for cookies or lemonade, or shelter from a sudden shower. It was still just the same.

The air was warm and steamy, laden with sweet and spicy and coffee smells. Everything was shining clean, but wonderfully cluttered. The oilcloth-covered table was strewn with green and half-ripe tomatoes. On the open oven door a shoebox emitted a piercing sound that Cindy recognized.

She almost ran across the room and knelt to look into the box. Baby chicks, at this time of the year! There were two of them, fluffy yellow, huddled tightly together in a corner of the box and cheeping at the tops of their voices.

"Cindy!" Mrs. Nichols' voice was warm with welcome. Her round face beamed with delight as she hurried into the room. She circled Cindy with one arm, while with the other she held out the blue and white gingham dress. It hung from a hanger, and was crisply ironed and neatly mended.

"We'll put this right here for you." She hooked the hanger over an empty dishtowel rack, and bent to pick up the shoebox with the chicks inside. "Imagine a hen silly enough to hide her nest this time of year, and then lead the babies right into the middle of my chrysanthemums. When Ted went out to water them for me, the way he does every day since it's been so dry, they got soaked. I think they're dried out enough now, don't you? Would you mind taking them out and putting them with their mother? I shut her in a coop, out by the garden fence."

"I'll be glad to, Mrs. Nichols." All Cindy's embarrassment had gone. It was as if she had been here only yesterday. She held each chick against her cheek for a moment before she set it down gently inside the coop and watched it run for the shelter of its mother's wings. They were so light, so soft and frail to have such big voices. They were so young, two days old at most, and yet they had clamored unceasingly until they got their way. Now they had gotten it, and they were quiet.

Back inside the kitchen, Cindy found that in the few minutes she had been gone Mrs. Nichols had cleared the table. Now it was set with a steaming cup of coffee and one of cocoa. Fat, heavily sugared doughnuts heaped a platter in the center.

"Sit down, Cindy. I know you like cocoa. Help yourself to doughnuts."

Cindy's mouth watered, but she hesitated. "You shouldn't have bothered, Mrs. Nichols. I had lunch."

"Still, you can eat. You're a growing girl," Mrs. Nichols insisted.

Cindy needed no more urging. She ate three doughnuts, tender and sweet and still warm. She finished the cocoa, three cups. Then she sighed blissfully.

"Thank you," she said. "And thanks for fixing the dress. I wouldn't have asked you myself, but Ted said you wouldn't mind. It was my fault it was so bad. I shouldn't have worn it after it was ripped, but I couldn't find anything else for school. I guess I'm growing a lot. Everything is getting too tight to button, or else so short I'm ashamed to be seen in it."

Mrs. Nichols looked her up and down. "Yes, you've grown. I figured you had, so I let down your hem while I was about it. But you still look as if a stiff breeze would blow you away. You've got plenty of growing to do yet. You gather up the rest of those dresses and bring them over here the first chance you get. I'll see if there's any hems I can let down, or seams I can let out. Ted tells me you can't sew a stitch. I'll bet you can't cook or clean, either."

Cindy hung her head. She could feel her face growing hot. "No, ma'am."

"Now, I didn't mean to make you feel bad about it." Mrs. Nichols leaned across the table and patted her hand. "You learned what you needed to know. On a farm, unless there's plenty of other help, the oldest pitches in with the outside chores. I know, because I was the oldest in my family. You might not believe it, Cindy, but I never did learn to sew or cook until after I was married. My! It's a good thing Mr. Nichols had plenty of patience and a strong stomach."

Cindy giggled. It was hard to believe, but very comforting.

"Don't know what I'd have done, if I'd been left on my own at your age." Mrs. Nichols shook her head. "Same as you, I suppose. But it's no wonder if you haven't anything fit to wear. And what happened to your hair? Cut it yourself?"

Cindy said apologetically, "It was hanging in my eyes."

"And your father wouldn't notice if you looked like a shaggy sheepdog. You couldn't remind him to take you to the barber's, I suppose?"

Cindy didn't answer. There didn't seem to be anything to say.

Mrs. Nichols eyed her thoughtfully, with her head on one side. "Those bangs are going to be in your eyes again in a day or two. Just you wait a minute." She bustled out of the room and returned with her hands full of small objects.

"Here's a couple of barrettes I got one time and never used. Now, you just take this hair and pull it up like this and fasten it—see? My, I wish I had your hair! You're right to want to grow it longer. It's got a nice little natural curl, but you've got to help it along. Just dampen it and curl it over your finger like this. Then if you want to tie a ribbon around, like this. Now, isn't that pretty?"

While she talked, Mrs. Nichols had been busy deftly combing and patting at Cindy's hair, and finishing off with a narrow blue ribbon. She held up a hand mirror for Cindy to look at herself.

Cindy would hardly have recognized her own face. She looked older, softer, prettier. But after a moment she frowned and looked away. "I haven't got time for all that foolishness."

Mrs. Nichols looked a little hurt. But after a moment she said cheerfully, "No, I guess you haven't. But don't you forget to bring those dresses over. Then if you can find time to sit down with me for an hour or so I'll teach you how to handle a needle and thread. Anybody ought to know how to put on a button or sew up a rip. Anybody, man or woman. Believe me, I've made my boys learn. Maybe I wouldn't have, if we'd had a girl in the family. Always did wish I had one, to help me out and keep me company around the house. Not but what the boys are very good to help, and do anything I ask them to. But a mother can't fuss over them, the way she can over a girl. Now, I'd just love to sit down and make a pretty dress for a girl. How about it, Cindy, wouldn't you like me to make one for you?"

Cindy said stiffly: "I couldn't let you do that. Dad wouldn't like it. He didn't even like it much when Grandma sent me two new dresses just before school started. He didn't say so, but I think he was glad when we found out they were too small for me to wear. He wouldn't let me mention it to Grandma when I wrote to thank her, so she could change them for bigger ones. They're just hanging in the closet now, wasted."

"What a shame!" Mrs. Nichols shook her head. "Still, maybe I can fix them up for you. Or if not, Marcella will grow into them in a couple of years. But, Cindy, your father's got to face facts. If he's too proud to let anybody give you clothes, he'll have to buy you some. He ought to see how badly you need them. But if he doesn't, you'll just have to tell him."

In stubborn misery, Cindy shook her head. "I can't. And please, don't say anything to him about it, Mrs. Nichols. I can manage."

Mrs. Nichols said, "Hmph! No fear of that. Not that I wouldn't like to give him a good piece of my mind, and not that I'd be afraid to. But it's not my business. It's yours, and his. I declare, though, I'm amazed. I always thought Dave Martin was a fine man, and good to his family, even if he was independent as a hog on ice when it came to outsiders. I'm surprised to find you scared to talk to him."

"Oh, no!" Cindy cried. "It's not that."

"Then what is it, for heaven's sake?" Cindy bit her lip and said nothing. But after a moment she saw Mrs.

Nichols' face soften. Quickly she rose and came around the table. She put her warm, soft arm around Cindy's shoulder.

For a moment Cindy let herself lean against the comforting bulk of Mrs. Nichols. She wished she were much younger, young enough to let go and cry. Then she drew away.

Mrs. Nichols looked at her tenderly, and dabbed at her eyes with a crumpled handkerchief. "Of course, Cindy! I should have known. It's just that you don't want to worry your father about money, with all his other troubles. I suppose I didn't realize you'd grown up enough to be that unselfish. It's a fine thing that you're so willing to help him.

"All of his neighbors would like to help, too, if they only could. We've seen the things he's had to do. Like selling that pretty little touring car he was so proud of and used to keep shined up so nice. And letting the dairy herd go. That was the worst of all. I almost cried when I heard he'd done that. Mr. Nichols and I did a lot of figuring, thinking maybe we could manage to loan him enough to tide him over. But everything we could scrape together wouldn't have helped much, and we decided that if we offered it he'd never take it. He's so determined not to take any favors."

"He's right, too," Cindy said proudly. "A man's got to stand on his own feet, and take care of his own family. I'm the only one who can help."

"And you have helped," Mrs. Nichols assured her warmly. "I don't know what he'd have done without you. Not many girls would have pitched in the way you did. Many a time I've seen you from my window last summer, in the heat of the sun, riding the cultivator all day behind that white team. I know you've done about every job there is—shocked wheat, pitched hay, and all."

"But I like to," Cindy insisted. "I only wish I didn't have to go to school. Then I could do more now than just milking and feeding."

"You do enough," Mrs. Nichols said. "The worry and the doing without is the worst, I know. Plenty of folks think your father's been foolish not to let the Ellsworths help with all those bills. After all, they're your family, too."

Cindy didn't answer. She didn't know what to say. She had mentioned help from Grandma and Grandpa once herself, when things had seemed particularly difficult. The look her father had given her had made her very careful never to mention it again.

Apparently Mrs. Nichols had found her own answer. She said, "I guess I know how he feels. Maybe he's foolish, but you're right to be proud of him. He's a man. And you're like him, just the kind of daughter he needs."

No other words could have filled Cindy with more pride, or with more shame. Pride, because there was no higher praise than to tell her she was like her father. Shame, because she didn't deserve it, and because she wasn't brave enough to admit to Mrs. Nichols that she didn't deserve it.

Mrs. Nichols thought it was unselfish consideration for her father that made her keep silent. But she knew it wasn't. Cindy knew she would have gone hungry or cold, endured any hardship she could imagine, rather than ask her father for money. But not for any noble, unselfish reason. For a reason that would seem foolish to Mrs. Nichols, or to anyone.

Asking her father for money would remind him that there was an easy way to get some. It would start him thinking about selling Tom and Sade.

8 : A Sad Decision

Cindy had just hung the mended dress in her closet when she heard her father come into the house. She ran downstairs, and found him waiting for her in the kitchen. He looked even older and more tired than he had in the truck coming home from town.

"Cindy," he said slowly, "I guess you couldn't help hearing what Mr. Sands said to me at the bank."

Cindy said, "I heard it."

"We've done our best. We've worked hard. You've helped more than I thought anybody your age could. We've done without everything we could spare and still keep going. And still we can't pay what we owe. Do you think it's right to turn down money?"

Cindy wished she didn't know what he meant by that. But she did know, and knew there was only one answer, and that she had to say it. The word seemed to stab her throat as it came out. "No."

Her father's voice was soft and husky. "Ben Thompson's not a cruel man. He doesn't abuse his animals. He's stingy, but not stingy enough to let them want. They'd really be better off with him. He's got good barns and pasture, plenty of feed. And he lives so close, you could see them sometimes."

Cindy swallowed hard. "I—I guess they wouldn't

really miss me much, anyway. As long as they're to-gether they'll get along all right."

"Of course they will!" Dave Martin reached out to rumple Cindy's hair. "You don't have to worry."

When he had gone, Cindy dropped into a chair with her back to the door and her elbows propped on the table. A lump in her throat swelled until she seemed to have no room left to breathe.

In all the empty house there was no sound but the lonely ticking of the clock. Cindy just sat there, feeling as if she never wanted to move again. Another of the things she loved was going away, and there was nothing she could do about it. There was nothing she could do about anything, no matter how hard she tried. Nothing she did could change the way things happened, any more than the ticking of that stupid clock could change the way the time kept going by.

But all that ticking wasn't just the clock. There was a louder, less regular ticking behind her. Slowly, she turned her head to look.

It was Mrs. Pickins, the Martins' oldest hen. As Cindy watched, she pecked impatiently at the screen door. Again there was the ticking noise, as her beak struck the wire. Behind Mrs. Pickins the rest of the flock, plump red hens and a few stately roosters, stood watch-ing. They were silent as statues, their heads cocked alertly on one side, their bright eyes intent upon the door.

They looked so funny that Cindy couldn't help laugh-ing, and at once she felt much better. She had been sit-ting here feeling sorry for herself because Dad was going to sell her team, and that made her feel helpless and unimportant.

Being the most important person in the world to eighty-seven chickens might not be much, but it was better than nothing. When they came home in the evening to find no water in their pans, it was Cindy Martin who could make everything right, and they had come to find her.

Opening the door, she restored the statues to life. They crowded around her with imploring squawks, pressing so close that she could hardly walk.

Fending off chickens while she pumped, wading knee-deep in chickens on her way, Cindy carried two pails of water for the drinking pans, and then a pail of cracked corn from the shed. She flung the corn about in handfuls, while the chickens scratched for it with delighted cluckings and croonings. Then she dashed for the henhouse to search the nests for eggs.

She was glad there were no setting hens installed in any of the nests. She dreaded their stubborn defiance, the way they had of ruffling their feathers and threatening her with their sharp, half-open yellow beaks. Of course she knew that their pecking wouldn't really hurt her. Usually it didn't even break the skin. Still, she always wished she could turn and run away.

There were nineteen eggs, which went into the pail. And of course there would be more. Only dull, unimaginative hens laid their eggs in the henhouse nests. The lively and adventurous ones found more interesting places, where they hoped to keep them hidden until they could be secretly hatched into chicks. It was one of

Cindy's jobs to find them while they were still fresh, because too many things could happen to hidden nests. The eggs could be broken, spoiled, eaten by all sorts of animals from rats up to her own Tom, or if it was winter they could be frozen. Even if hatched, the chicks would be like the two she had seen over at the Nichols' place, too few, coming into a world unprepared to give them the care they needed.

Busy with their food and water, the hens didn't follow Cindy as she headed back to the house. She took the pail of eggs into the pantry and put them carefully into the big crate. Two cracked ones she put into a bowl on the shelf to be used at home.

There was a pail of skim milk on the back porch, and beside it another pail half full of table scraps. Cindy picked up the pails, the milk in her right hand because it was heavier, the scraps in her left. She walked as fast as she could toward the hoghouse, but twice she had to set down her load to ease the pain of the wire bails cutting into her palms.

At the top of the hill in front of the barn, she began to whistle a piercing imitation of the Army mess call. All over the feedlot, pigs emerged from their napping places deep in the clumps of tall jimson weed and burdock, and raced for the troughs outside the hoghouse door. There they stood with hoofs planted on the lowest board of the fence, eager snouts poked as far between as the narrow space would allow, and squealed in frenzied entreaty.

As Cindy lifted the pails and poured their contents into the troughs she was breathless, partly from exertion and partly from whistling. But she grinned triumphantly. Most people thought you had to call pigs with the same old, monotonous "Sooie." She'd proved you didn't.

The milk splashed into one trough, the scraps into the other. By the time Cindy had made a trip to the well, and back again with pails of water, they were empty.

The corncrib was nearly empty. Cindy searched the corners for an armful of ears and pitched them, one at a time, out through the window into the feed lot. She threw hard and straight, aiming each ear at a different angle so that they would land in widely separated places.

When she came out, the pigs were crunching away contentedly, each at his own ear of corn. All but a single unlucky one, who ran about frantically, squealing protests and making futile snatches at his neighbors' corn. At last he found an ear for himself, and seized it eagerly.

Cindy leaned against the fence to watch. The pigs were half grown, their solid, brick-red bodies still slim enough for quick movement. They ate quietly, with only occasional soft grunts of pleasure. Their tight-curled tails jerked and quivered with delight.

One of them finished his ear of corn and gave the empty cob a shove with his pink snout. He was one of the few Cindy could pick out from the bunch, the biggest of them all. He shook himself and strolled toward Cindy.

Some water had splashed from the trough and collected into a small puddle near the fence. The pig sniffed at it for a moment, then turned and dropped flat on his side. He lay stretched at full length, wriggling himself slowly into the soft mud. From deep in his throat came sounds like a harsh and jerky sort of purring.

Cindy reached through the fence to scratch behind his ear. The sounds quickened and increased, until they were like the noise the truck made when it struggled to start on a cold morning.

"Hey, Cindy! You must like pigs." It was Ted looking down at her, his hands in his pockets.

"Hi," Cindy said. "Sure I do. They're smart. This one's named Goliath. Because he's so big, you know."

Ted wrinkled his nose. "I can see keeping hogs for the money they bring in, but I can't see making pets out of them. They're so dirty. My father says they're the biggest pests alive, always trying to get out, and into some place where they shouldn't be."

"You can't call them dirty just because they like to wallow in mud," Cindy answered. "That's the way they keep cool. Keeps the flies off, too. Didn't you ever see one making his bed up for the night?"

Ted shook his head. "Do they? I never noticed."

"Sure they do. You just watch some time. They'll fluff up the straw—or the cornhusks or leaves, or whatever they have to sleep on—with their noses. And they'll rake out anything that doesn't belong there and get rid of it. They're very particular. And of course they try to get out. That only shows how smart they are. Wouldn't you want to get out if somebody shut you up in a pen?"

"Well— Yes, I guess so. But how about the way they eat? When you say a person is making a pig of himself, you're not paying him a compliment."

"And you're not being fair, either," Cindy said hotly. "Did you ever hear of a pig eating enough to make himself sick? I never did. You know you can't turn a horse or a cow loose in a cornfield. It would eat enough to kill itself. But a pig will just take as much as he needs, and then stop. I'll bet that's more than you'd do, or me either, if somebody turned us loose in a candy store."

Ted laughed. "All right, I give up. The whole world misjudges pigs. They're all perfect ladies and gentlemen."

"Well," Cindy admitted, "not quite. I must say, they're pretty pigheaded. Now, that's an expression that really does fit them. Try to keep a pig away from something he wants, and you've really got your hands full. And of course they're not easy to handle. They don't follow the leader, like sheep. Every one's got a mind of his own."

"I thought maybe I could help you with your chores," Ted said. "Didn't know all you had to do was stand around and talk about pigs."

Cindy stiffened. "I never asked you to come over and help."

"Well, of course not," Ted agreed amiably. "I just thought it would be fun. If I was home, Mom would be asking me to peel potatoes for supper, or some sissy job like that."

Cindy giggled. "Can't blame you, then. Want to help milk?"

"Sure. I'll get the pails. On the porch, aren't they?"

Cindy stood, unexpectedly idle and empty-handed, and watched the cows ambling up the lane.

"Don't they look like two fat ladies strolling to church on Sunday?" she asked Ted when he had joined her. "Too bad they don't decide to go back to the pasture. I love to see how fast Shep can show up if they make a wrong move. You don't think he's anywhere around, but those cows wouldn't take half a dozen steps before he'd be after them."

Ted scanned the lane, the orchard, everything in sight. "He sure doesn't seem to be around this time," he said.

"Wait and see." Cindy whistled, and the dog appeared in the lane as instantly as a rabbit whisked from a magician's hat. Ignoring the placid cows, he eased past them and then broke into a run. He squeezed through the narrow gap beside the watering trough, and leaped at Cindy. With his paws on her shoulders, his long pink tongue reaching for her face, he waved his bushy tail wildly and uttered small, ecstatic squeaks of greeting. Cindy hugged him once, and then said sternly, "Down!"

Shep dropped instantly to all fours. He looked so apologetic that Cindy had to kneel beside him and hug him once more to show him she wasn't cross.

"You are the best dog in the whole world."

The smile faded from Ted's face. He said softly, *"Now* he is, maybe." Cindy knew he was remembering Lady, Shep's mother. She had been like one of the Nichols family for years, and had died only a few months before. For Ted, Lady had been the best dog in the world. Maybe every dog was the best dog in the world, for somebody.

Looking at Shep as impartially as she could, Cindy had to admit that he would never have taken any ribbons in a dog show. Considered as a specimen of collie, he was too broad for his height. His nose was broad and blunt, his forehead too wide. His coat, which was spotted in white, black, and several shades of brown, was coarse and shaggy.

But looks weren't important. The important thing was the way Shep worked. Without being told, he fetched the cows from the pasture every day, morning and evening. He did it always at the proper time, as if he had a very accurate alarm clock inside his head. If he were following Cindy's father about the fields when the time came, or sleeping, or even chasing a rabbit, he would suddenly pull himself together, give himself a little shake, and set off for the pasture. That was his job, the only job for which he felt responsible.

He was good at getting in strays, and would take charge of any animal he found out of its proper place without being told, driving it as near the barn as he could and then barking until someone came to take charge. But he kept no special watch for them. He battled rats, foxes, or any other strange beast that crossed his path, but he didn't go out of his way to look for them. As a watchdog, he was no use at all. Everyone human was his friend. Cindy and her father agreed that if burglars ever broke into their house, Shep would probably help them carry away their loot.

While the cows were still at the watering trough drinking, their two calves came frolicking up the lane, kicking up great clouds of dust with their pointed hoofs.

Cindy and Ted shooed the cows into the barn before
the calves had time to follow, and quickly closed the
door behind them. Scampie, the red bull calf, butted
the door a couple of times and bawled his resentment.
But Mitzi, the trim, fawn-colored heifer, turned and
walked daintily back to the watering trough and stood on
tiptoe, her neck stretched to drink. After a moment
Scampie followed her.

The cows went to their stanchions at the opposite
ends of the barn, the stanchions they had become accustomed to when there was a herd to be milked. Cindy's
father had filled the shallow mangers with hay that
morning, and so they began to eat at once.

"You'd better take Maisie," Cindy told Ted. The
big red-and-white Shorthorn was an easy milker with
a placid disposition, and not likely to protest at being
touched by a stranger. Daisy, the young Jersey, fidgeted
and kicked even for Cindy.

Shep sat watching Cindy, but at a respectful distance
from Daisy's heels. He was panting, his long red tongue
hanging out of his mouth. As the milk began to drum
against the bottom of the pails, cats appeared silently,
one by one. At last there were eight of them, all white,
all with bright, expectant blue eyes. There was a battered old tom, a weary-looking mother with four small
kittens, and two slim, half-grown youngsters. They
clustered around Cindy, the kittens wailing imploringly, the old tom mewing impatiently, the others silent.

Ted rattled his pail invitingly, and they ran toward
him. Laughing, he squirted a jet of milk at the big cat's

open mouth. It missed his mouth and sprayed his chest
and face. He led the procession back to Cindy's end
of the barn, then sat down and began to wash himself
indignantly.

When Cindy could stop laughing, she said, "Shame
on you, Ted Nichols! How'd you like to have somebody
do that to you?"

"Somebody has. All my brothers, several times
apiece."

"Yes, but I don't suppose you really minded. Cats get
so embarrassed."

"Honest, Cindy!" Ted shook his head. "You're always talking about animals as if they were people. Little
kids do things like that, but I should think you'd have
outgrown it."

"I—" Cindy glared at him, and started to deny it.
But then she realized it was true. While she poured milk
into the two battered pie tins that were kept in the
corner for Shep and the cats, she thought about it.
Surely there was nothing wrong with thinking about
animals as if they were people. But now it did seem
rather childish. And childish was the last thing Cindy
wanted to be.

She had wanted to call Ted's attention to the way
Shep and the cats ate side by side, with neither trying
to take anything from the others, just like good neighbors. But now she couldn't say it. In thoughtful silence,
she went back to finish her milking.

Ted reached for her pail as they started to leave the
barn. Fighting down her instinct to protest, Cindy let
him have it. It gave her a strange feeling when he stood

back to let her go through the door first. It wasn't like Ted.

All their lives they had raced, competed, argued. They hadn't been rude to each other. They had shared fairly, taken equal turns. Neither would willingly have let the other be hurt. They had been apart for most of a year, and now Ted had come back strangely different in his ways.

Suddenly she realized what it was. Ted was treating her like a lady. That was why he had offered her his hand on the path that night. That was why he hadn't wrestled with her in the water, the way he used to do, but only laughed while he held her off. She wanted to shout at him to stop it. Everything had been happy and wonderful before. There was no need to change. But she had a feeling that nothing she said would make any difference.

She broke into a hard run, slammed open the cellar door, scrambled down the steps. She clattered the crocks and the strainers, made a great banging of cupboard doors as if she were looking for something, although there was really nothing more she needed. Anything to keep from looking at Ted, or from having to speak to him.

She wanted to finish with the milk and escape. And at the same time she didn't want to leave. She wondered why she had ever thought this cellar frightening. Now it seemed like a refuge, snug and secure.

9 : Good News—Twice

Cindy was just starting up the cellar steps when she saw that there was someone standing just outside. It was Ben Thompson, looking like a pathetic old tramp in his shabby overalls and worn-out shoes. Because he walked everywhere and there was no sound of engine or of horses' hoofs or rattling wheels to warn of his approach, seeing him was usually a surprise. Even Shep didn't bark at the sight of him, because he had been here so often.

Cindy stopped short, and then took a step back, almost bumping into Ted who was following close behind her. "Sh!" she whispered. "It's that old Ben Thompson. Let's go up the other way so we won't have to see him."

They groped their way through the dimness of an inner room to the stairway that went up inside, into the kitchen.

Ted said, "What's the matter? I feel silly, running away like this. Why are you scared of Ben Thompson?"

"I'm not! I hate him. Dad's going to sell him my— my team." Cindy's voice broke despairingly.

"Oh." Ted's face was solemn. "I'm sorry. But I know your father wouldn't, unless he needed the money badly. So why be mad at Ben Thompson? He might as well buy them as anybody else. At least, they'll still be close, and you'll know they're all right."

"I know all that. Dad said the very same thing. But it's not just because he's buying them. I wouldn't hate him if he really wanted them. But all he wants is to make Dad sell something he doesn't want to sell."

"That's silly," Ted scoffed. "Why should he want to do that?"

"I don't know," Cindy admitted.

"Cindy," Ted said in a serious voice, "I guess I know how you feel. That team is something special to you, the way our dog Lady was to me. When she died—I never told anybody, but I'll tell you. I cried. Hid out in the hayloft and cried just like a baby. I think that's what you'd really like to do now. You'd feel better, maybe, if you did."

Cindy shook her head. "Crying never did anybody any good."

"You're wrong," Ted said gently. "There are times when it can do you a lot of good. Some things you can't fight, you can't do anything about. Like when Lady died, I was mad. I wanted to fight somebody. But nobody was to blame. There was nothing I could do. There was no place for the fight in me to go, and the crying let it come out so it didn't do anybody any harm. Afterward I could think. I could realize that we just can't count on animals being with us forever. They aren't like people."

"They're better!" Cindy said fiercely. "You never know what to expect from people. They change their minds, break promises, turn their backs on you just when you need them. Animals don't. You can depend on them."

"Now, Cindy!" Ted touched her shoulder in an awkward attempt at comfort. "You're just human yourself, you know. Maybe your friends did turn their backs on you once. But you've turned yours on them plenty of times since. Mag Keller tells me you go around with your nose in the air at school, and nobody can get a civil word out of you. Says you wouldn't even go to the weiner roast the eighth grade had last week. She tells me Miss Emery was pretty disappointed, too. She'd tried so hard to arrange so everybody could come."

"I was sorry about that," Cindy admitted. "I like Miss Emery. She asked me to be on the committee to plan the games. But why should I go? I can't stand those kids any more. They've all turned so silly. All the girls want to do is comb their hair and talk about their new clothes. And boys!" Cindy brought out the last sentence in a tone of biting contempt.

"Well!" Ted looked at her with exaggerated surprise. "So, boys are human too, aren't they?"

Cindy couldn't help giggling. "All right! So I have nothing against sensible boys like you. But why do they have to be so mushy about it? And those boys in my class are nearly as bad as the girls. Showing off, and hanging around after people like Susie Miller. Pretending she's scared to death of spiders, and I suppose she thinks we can't remember that just last year she was collecting them."

"Oh, come on, Cindy!" Ted said more seriously. "Don't be so hard on those kids. My father says that's just a natural part of growing up. You know how a young rooster gets overgrown and scrawny and awkward for a while. Humans have to go through the same kind of stage. You don't go overnight from being a little kid to being a grown-up person. You have to get used to it. Maybe you're a little later getting around to that stage than your friends. But you'll have to go through it, too."

"I won't!" Cindy cried. "I wish I could be like Peter Pan and never grow up at all."

Ted shook his head sympathetically. "Miss Ramsey, our English teacher, says lots of people must wish that, and that's why the book was so popular. She says the reason for it is fear and laziness."

"She's crazy!" Cindy's voice was taut with fury. "I'd like to see her out here, just one day. I'll bet I'd wear her out. And scare her to death, too."

"That's not the way she means it," Ted explained patiently. "When you're grown up you've got to make up your own mind about things, decide what's best to do, and when you're wrong you've got to take the blame. Lots of people are afraid to do that, or they don't want to bother. It's more comfortable to have somebody take care of them, and tell them what to do. Sometimes people even try to go backward, as some children when they get a little sister or brother, they start acting like babies again. Even wanting to drink out of a bottle, or be rocked to sleep. They're trying to put things back the way they were before, because it's uncomfortable to have them changed. But of course nobody can."

Cindy had grown so interested that she forgot about

being angry. "Do you really talk about that kind of stuff in high school? I think I'm going to like it."

"Oh, not all the time," Ted admitted. "We have to write compositions, and learn the rules of grammar, and all that. But Miss Ramsey says the main reason we study English is so we can communicate with other people. She says we're just wasting our time if it doesn't help us understand one another's ideas and feelings better."

Voices sounded outside. Footsteps came across the porch. Ted said, "I'd better be going. See you tomorrow, Cindy. Mom said if your father goes to see your mother, why don't you eat dinner with us. Will you?"

"Why— Yes, I guess so. Thanks."

Cindy's father looked down the walk after Ted, who had left with a hurried greeting just as he and Ben Thompson came in. "What did he want?"

"Nothing. He was helping me with my chores."

"There's no need—" her father began angrily. Then he stopped and looked at Cindy thoughtfully. "But then I suppose there's no harm either, if he really wants to."

Then he turned to Ben Thompson. "All right. I've finally made up my mind to sell. A hundred and a half was your last price. You're getting a good team."

Now that the words were said, Cindy had a feeling almost of relief. Now it was decided. Much as she still dreaded the thought of the empty stall, she knew this was the only right and honest thing to do. She wished the money was paid and the horses gone. Then there would be nothing to do but make the best of it.

"Team? What are you talking about?" Ben Thompson's voice sounded puzzled. Cindy was filled with a wild and joyful amazement. He had changed his mind. Her team was safe. She wanted to leap and yell with delight.

"Team?" Ben said again. "How did you get the idea I wanted to buy the team? All I want's the gelding. Got the match to him at home. White gelding, like him as another pea out of the same pod. Took him on a debt."

Cindy froze with horror. Surely she couldn't have heard that right. Not even Ben Thompson could say so calmly anything so awful as that. She glanced up at her father. He looked as unbelieving as she felt.

"You said—just the gelding? That's all you want?"

"He's the only one I ever wanted. Thought you knew that."

Dave Martin shook his head. "Sorry, Ben. I don't believe in breaking up a team. Take them both, and it's a deal."

The old man snorted. "Wouldn't have that mare if you paid me for her keep. Don't know why you ever ruined a good work horse, teaming him up with a blind mare. I'll put him with a sound, healthy partner. Wind up with a team that amounts to something."

Relief flowed over Cindy in a warm tide. All her worry had been for nothing. Of course her father wouldn't break up the team. They had always been together, and they always would be. Nobody but cold, miserly old Ben Thompson could even have thought of separating them. If only her father had known what

Ben was after, he'd have refused in words that would have told him it was no use coming back.

But even now Ben wasn't through. He went on coaxingly. "I know you can use the money, Dave. This has been a bad year. Not a man in the county's got decent crops, with the weather we've had. And it's hit you extra hard on top of your other troubles. I don't hardly see how you can afford to turn down a chance like this."

Cindy gazed up at her father imploringly. She saw his eyes waver, saw him swallow hard and bite his lip. "You're right, Ben. It's been a tough year. But—I just can't sell that gelding. The mare's been raised with him. He's been her eyes all her life. I couldn't part them."

Ben Thompson chuckled, a dry, creaking sound. "Never thought you were fool enough to let sentiment stand between you and a good trade, Dave. Still can't believe you really are. You think about it a while. If you decide to be sensible, just bring the horse over to my place. I'll have the cash ready."

"Sure, Ben. I'll think about it. Have to admit your price is fair." Cindy heard embarrassment in her father's voice, and knew he was sorry for what he had said about the team. He would never have said it, except that he had been shocked and taken by surprise. People might feel soft things like love or fear or pity, but they didn't talk about them. Once they were past being babies, they hid them. Still, she knew he wouldn't be embarrassed enough to change his mind. The team was safe. Cindy could have shouted for happiness.

Ben turned away, then quickly back. "Almost forgot

to give you this. Mail carrier gave it to me when I met him down at the end of your lane." He reached into his pocket and pulled out an envelope, folded in half and smudged with grimy fingerprints.

Cindy's father reached for the envelope and, without looking at it, thrust it into his pocket. "Thanks."

Ben still hesitated. "By the way—how's the missus?"

Cindy glanced quickly at her father. The muscles along his jaw tightened. His shoulders hunched forward a little. She heard his breath loud and harsh, and saw Ben Thompson step quickly back. Then her father said softly, "She's coming along. She'll be home soon as she's able."

"Fine! Glad to hear it," Ben squeaked. He scurried out into the dimness.

Shivering with impatience, Cindy watched her father take out the envelope. His hands shook a little as he tore open the flap, unfolded the letter and read quickly through it. Then he sat down, spread the paper flat on the table and slowly read it again.

She had known the moment Ben Thompson took it out of his pocket that the letter was from her mother. Soiled and crumpled as it was, the square, pale-pink envelope was unmistakable. Now she knew the news in it was good. With each line her father read his face softened, the tired, driven look faded from his eyes, the tightness of his mouth relaxed. When he had finished he sat for a moment with eyes closed, a smile lifting the corners of his lips.

Cindy was half frightened, for it seemed that he had turned all at once into a stranger. Then she realized that this was the way he had looked a long time ago, before her mother went away.

At last he said, "Cindy, your mother's left the hospital. She's at Grandpa's. Shall we go see her tomorrow?"

It was so much better than Cindy had expected, even though she had known the news was good, that for a moment she couldn't speak. Coming on top of the happiness over Tom and Sade, this new joy overwhelmed her. She felt a sort of shivering inside, as if she had suddenly turned to jelly, bones and all. She groped for a chair, let herself slowly down onto it, and finally managed to find her voice. "Can we really see her?"

She hadn't seen her mother for almost a year, because the hospital didn't allow anyone under sixteen to visit. Her father had explained that the rule wasn't so much because children might catch something from the patients. It was mostly because children often carried the germs of colds or measles or such things and might pass them on to the patients, who had enough trouble already.

Cindy understood that, and knew that it was best. But she had to remind herself of it again each Sunday as she stood and watched her father drive away in the truck. He looked stiff and strange in a white shirt and a necktie, but there was always an eager, hopeful expression on his face.

Through the long, lonesome day she waited, glad if there was weeding or hoeing or any outside job to do to make the time go faster. At evening she listened impatiently for the sound of the truck. She was always happy when she could run to meet her father, yet she dreaded to see his face after each trip. He always looked tired and cross.

She wouldn't have minded his looking tired. That was to be expected, after his long trip. What she dreaded was to see him looking cross, because that meant he was worried and afraid. It meant her mother still wasn't well, still didn't know how long it would be before she could come home.

But that was all over now. Happiness glowed on her father's face, and sang in his voice. The quivery weakness inside Cindy was suddenly gone. She jumped up and threw her arms around her father, hugging him tight, burying her face against the roughness of his shirt. And he was hugging her, his arms strong as iron, squeezing her until she could hardly breathe.

Cindy stiffened and drew away. Sudden happiness, and the strength of her father's arms, had brought tears to her eyes. She had almost made him ashamed of her, crying like a silly baby.

"Guess it's time we had some supper," she said abruptly.

Cindy scurried around setting the table. Her father whistled as he built up the fire and put things on to cook. He whistled "Tipperary" and then "Dixie." After that he started "In the Gloaming," which was her mother's favorite song. But he broke that off in the middle of a long, quavering note, and after a moment went back to "Tipperary." Cindy listened blissfully. She had always loved to hear her father whistle, and this was the first chance she'd had in a long, long time.

The whistling, and the smell of frying onions, filled

the room and made it seem cozy and warm. When they sat down to eat, she was too happy to notice that the onions were scorched and the scrambled eggs half raw.

Looking at her father across the table, she remembered Ben Thompson and laughed. It was strange to think how she had hated him. Now he was just funny.

"Why did you get so mad at Mr. Thompson?" she asked. "I thought you were going to hit him. I guess he did too, the way he jumped."

Her father laughed. "The old codger has been trying his best to get on my nerves. Don't know why I ever let him bother me."

Cindy frowned, puzzled. "I wondered before. You never liked it when he asked about Mama. Why?"

"Well—" He laughed in an embarrassed way. "I suppose there's no harm in telling you. Did you know Ben had a wife once?"

Cindy's mouth dropped open in amazement. She shook her head.

"It was a long time ago. He was young then. From what I hear, his wife was a pretty woman and a nice one. Ben must have thought a lot of her. One day she went away and never came back."

"Really?" Cindy's voice was shocked, almost unbelieving. Married people didn't just go away from each other. They were like one person, as inseparable as a team of horses. You said their names in the same breath, and it was impossible to imagine one of them without the other.

Her father went on. "People said it happened about a parlor rug. Of course it didn't, really. That was prob-

ably just the last of a lot of troubles between them. I
suppose the real one was, they were both too stubborn
to pull together the way a married couple has to. Anyway, Ben's wife wanted to buy the rug and Ben
wouldn't give her the money, though he had enough
for twenty of them. So people figured Ben was an old
skinflint, and they didn't blame his wife. But Ben would
never admit he was wrong. He's been telling people
ever since that women can't be trusted. That they'll
walk out on any man who hasn't enough money to suit
them."

"You mean when he kept asking you how Mama was
and when she was coming home—you mean he wanted
you to start thinking maybe she'd never come home at
all? Not even after she got well? That's silly. I don't
know why you paid any attention."

"I don't either, now." Dad's face was like a boy's,
Cindy thought, as he pushed away his plate and leaned
back in his chair. Laugh lines at the corners of his lips
had replaced the deep frown she had grown used to
seeing. Even his voice was young. Words came out
easily and a little too fast, as if he had been stored full
of them for a long time and now they were all pouring
out at once. "I guess—well, maybe I thought it would
serve me right if she didn't ever come home. Before we
were married, your mother was used to nice things,
going places, having fun. She hasn't had much fun here.
Just hard work, lonesomeness, making do with the least
of everything. Even before she got sick, I wondered
sometimes how she could help being sorry she married
me."

"But she wasn't ever sorry!" Cindy protested. "She was always happy, always singing and laughing. Funny things were always happening when she was here."

Her father nodded. "I can remember those things now. But before, all I could think about were the bad things. Sometimes I thought she'd never get well. And then I thought, even if she did, she'd never be able to stand the sight of me again."

"But why shouldn't she?"

"Because I let her get so sick, and never even noticed anything was wrong. After it happened I could remember plenty of things that should have warned me she wasn't well." His voice was full of disgust for himself. "But she never said anything. If only she'd complained! If only she'd told me she didn't feel well."

Cindy was tempted to remind her father that he had never been the kind people felt like complaining to. Perhaps because he'd never known sickness himself, he believed that the best cure for any human ill was to ignore it. But she said nothing. If she did, it would only sound as if she were blaming him, and she didn't. He couldn't help being the way he was. He had been an orphan, brought up in the County Home for Children. There he must have learned very young that complaining was a fault and silent endurance a virtue.

She said comfortingly, "Mama knows you couldn't help it."

Her father's grin returned, and he settled himself back in his chair. "Anyway, things are turning out all right. She's well. She'll be coming home."

Cindy leaned forward eagerly. "Can we bring her tomorrow? And Davy and Marcy too!"

"I wouldn't count on that. Maybe not tomorrow. But soon. Any day now. And when she's home we can't let things be like they were before. We have to make things easy for her. She has to be the first one we think about."

When she was in bed, Cindy felt the way she always did on the night before Christmas. Tomorrow would be wonderful. Everything she had ever wished for would be waiting for her. Soon things would be the way they used to be. Tomorrow night—of course her father had said not to count on its being tomorrow night, but she was sure it would be—her mother would be here, sleeping in the room just down the hall. Marcy and Davy would be here, in their small and medium-sized beds at the other end of the room. If she woke in the night she would be able to hear their breathing and know she wasn't alone.

After tomorrow, when she came into the house it would be to cooking smells, to the sound of footsteps and voices, to the warmth and comfort of her mother's presence. All around, the farm would lie secure. Though they couldn't know why, surely every animal from Tom and Sade down to the youngest kitten would sleep more peacefully because they were safe.

There would be no more cherished things slipping away. Now the things that had been lost would start to come back again, little by little. Before long they would dare to dream and plan for new things, the way they used to.

10 : A Happy Journey

Morning coolness was still in the air when Cindy and her father left for Center City next day. They had hurried through the chores, hastily swallowed a cold breakfast, and rushed to dress for the trip.

At the last moment, Cindy remembered that she had promised to go to Ted's house for dinner. It would never do to ask her father to stop on the way to tell them she couldn't come. Center City was a three hours' drive in the truck, and they had to be home in time to start evening chores. At best, there would be little time to spend at Grandpa's.

So she hastily scribbled a note and pinned it to the screen door where Ted would be sure to see it if he should come over looking for her. It said, "Mama is all well and out of the hospital. We went to bring her home."

Shep ran beside the truck to the road, and as far along it as the pasture gate. When they kept going he stopped, and after a moment turned and trotted back toward the house.

Cindy sat up straight and gazed out the window. They were going north, away from the familiar road to Walnut Grove, and she didn't want to miss any of the sights. She counted the seasons backward, to remember how long ago her last trip on this road had been. More than four years!

It had been the Fourth of July. She remembered the flags out everywhere, and the noise of firecrackers. There had been only her parents and Marcy and herself in the car. There hadn't even been any Davy then. Marcy had been frightened at the noise of the firecrackers. Cindy smiled, remembering the way her little sister had pressed her hands to her ears and buried her face in her mother's lap. She could even remember what her mother and her father had been talking about as they drove along in the touring car, which had gone faster and made less noise than the truck.

Smoothing Marcy's tumbled yellow curls, Mama had said, "We must get away more often, Dave. The children are as scary as wild things fresh out of the woods."

She, Cindy, had interrupted indignantly, "Not me! I'm not scared."

Her mother had smiled. "Of course not, Cindy. You're big. You've been to school. I guess I really meant just Marcy."

After a little silence, her mother had gone on. "It's been three years, Dave. Remember how we planned to visit Dad and Mother twice a year? Christmas and the Fourth. And Decoration Day and Thanksgiving they'd come to see us. But it's been three years. I know it couldn't be helped. Something always happened. Once it was because Cindy had the measles. Then there was the time one of the cows was sick, and the time the car had a broken axle. But from now on we should do better."

Dad had answered, "Your folks haven't got children to keep them home. Or cows either."

"But there are other things. There was Dad's sprained ankle last fall. And then the time one of his managers was sick and he had to take over at the theater."

Dad had sounded a little cross. "Lucy, you know I do the best I can."

"Of course! I only meant— Well, Dad and Mother are the only family we have. The only relatives the children have in the world, besides us."

"The only relatives—" The words had surprised Cindy so much that she had never forgotten them. Remembering them always made her feel lonesome, and different from other people.

Everyone else had dozens of relatives. They had two sets of grandparents and often a great-grandparent or two. They had swarms of aunts and uncles, and multitudes of cousins. Walnut Grove was one great, tangled mass of relationships, where everyone was kin to everyone else. Other families had holiday dinners for thirty or forty, and family reunions where half the town spread basket lunches on the grass. Everyone but the Martins.

Cindy looked admiringly at her father. He was the one who really knew what it was to be alone. Dad never talked about his childhood in the County Home for Children, and though Cindy was curious about it she

never asked questions. Mama had told her that Dad
wanted only to forget his unhappy childhood.

Cindy wondered if it hadn't been even worse after
he had left the home, where at least there were other
children sharing the same life. Out in the lonesome
world, there would have been nobody to share with,
nobody to whom he meant anything, even as part of a
job. She wondered how he had been able to endure
being so alone.

She looked at him with a new understanding of the
tight lips and the square-set jaw. Stubborn independence must come naturally to someone who had never
had parents to depend on.

Cindy was startled out of her thoughts by a burst of
furious barking. A very small spotted dog was pursuing
them down the dusty main street of a town so much
smaller and shabbier than Walnut Grove that the
sight of it gave her a comfortable feeling of impor-
tance.

Now they began to meet people on the road, some in
cars, some in trucks, some in horse-drawn buggies or
surreys. They passed a church with people standing
about outside, talking in little groups while they waited
for someone to be the first to go in. Cindy felt a sudden
twinge of guilt.

When her mother was at home they had always gone
to church in Walnut Grove on Sunday mornings. Since
she'd been away they hadn't gone once. It wasn't that
Cindy had ever wished to go, even when the minister
had come right out into the field one day to say how
much he'd missed them. She'd been relieved when her

father told him curtly that they were too busy now, with her mother away in the hospital. It had been a relief to escape from the boredom of Sunday school and the torment of sitting quiet through the long sermon. But now that she saw all these scrubbed, starchily dressed people outside their church she knew that church was another thing she had missed.

Maybe going to church, even when you didn't want to, did something to you inside that you never knew about until you had been away from it for a long time. Maybe it was like the scrubbing and combing and fingernail cleaning you wished your mother wouldn't insist on every day.

The sun was high and hot by the time they came to the outskirts of Center City. Now there were new, different things to see. Big buildings, street cars, a flood of automobiles, hundreds of signs to read, people dressed in their best. Policemen blew shrill whistles. A street car rattled by, clanging a loud bell. Automobile horns blared. The cars whished by so fast and so close that she wondered how they always managed to miss the truck and each other.

They were passing store windows full of make-believe ladies and men and children beautifully dressed in new clothes. There were other windows arranged to look like rooms in a fine house. She saw a big window full of flowers in baskets and vases, and craned her neck to see whether they were real. Probably they were make-believe like the people, she thought. She had never seen any so big and so bright. There was a movie theater, immense, with big colored pictures outside.

One of the pictures was of a woman and a man kissing, and another was of two men fighting.

"Is that one of Grandpa's theaters?" Cindy asked excitedly.

Her father shook his head. "No. His are smaller. What they call neighborhood houses."

Just past the movie theater they turned into a quieter street, lined with houses. Cindy wished they were still on that busy street. She wished she had a whole day just to walk up and down it, looking at all the store windows, reading all the signs.

They turned into a wider street, divided into two sections by a grassy strip in the middle. On either side were elm trees so tall that their branches almost met overhead. Brick houses sat squarely behind neat lawns and well-kept flower beds, looking rich and smug. The dusty old truck seemed like a noisy intruder in such a grand neighborhood.

Cindy tried to remember which was her grandfather's house. The houses were all so much alike block after block. It would be dreadful to stop at the wrong one. But of course Dad would never make such a mistake.

At last they stopped. Dad said, "Well, here we are."

They got out and walked along a broad cement sidewalk which looked as if it had just been swept. Even this close, the grass beside it was perfect. Each blade was the same length, the same shade of green. It looked as if no foot had ever stepped on it.

Cindy's heart beat hard with happiness, with excitement, and with fear. In a few minutes she would see her mother. She wanted to run toward her as fast as she could. At the same time she wanted to run away. Now that she was so close, she realized that she had forgotten what her mother looked like.

She could tell anyone that her mother was tall and thin, that she had short dark hair that curled, dark eyes that looked too big for her face, cheeks with a bright flush of red like poppy petals. But she couldn't close her eyes and see the way her mother looked, as she had done so many nights just before she went to sleep.

She could tell anyone what her mother's voice was like, too. High and sweet, the words coming a little too fast, interrupted often by a breathless little burst of laughter and nearly as often by a harsh, rasping spasm of coughing. But she couldn't hear her mother's voice in her imagination. Maybe she wouldn't know her mother when she saw her, Cindy thought. Even worse, maybe after all this time her mother wouldn't know her.

Grandpa's house sat silent and aloof. No one opened a door or even looked out a window to see who had come, though someone must have heard the noise of the truck in the quiet street.

11 : Strangers in the City

Then Cindy and her father stood side by side at the front door of her grandfather's house. She looked up and saw that his face was hard, his jaw set, his eyebrows drawn together in a frown. She knew he was full of love, eagerness and hope. But he looked stern, almost threatening. Because he couldn't bear to have anyone see what he felt, and perhaps feel sorry for him.

Impulsively she tugged at his sleeve, wanting to tell him to smile. But when he looked down at her and said impatiently, "What is it, Cindy?" she lost her courage.

"I—I just wondered why you didn't ring the bell."

"I was about to." He punched the button hard, and she could hear ringing inside, too loud and too long for politeness.

Footsteps approached, getting louder. The door swung open. A tall, red-haired woman in a black dress and a white apron looked out at them, then beyond them at the truck. "Deliveries at the rear," she said.

Cindy's father took a step forward. He said in a low, harsh voice, "I'm here to see my wife. Mrs. Martin." The woman giggled, and tugged at the sides of her apron.

Cindy went hot with rage. This woman—this city

servant—was laughing at her. Worse than that, she
was laughing at her father.

But in a moment Grandpa Ellsworth was there, smiling and shaking Dad's hand, bending over to kiss
Cindy's cheek, scolding the woman for keeping company standing outside the door. Grandpa was just as
she remembered him, his face pink and shiny, his watch
chain gleaming across his fat stomach. His kiss brought
with it the familiar smell of cigars and shaving lotion.
Cindy's anger faded as they followed him across the
hall and into the living room. Her heart began to beat
faster as she looked about for her mother. But no one
was there.

She hadn't remembered before how the room looked.
But now that she was here, everything was familiar.
The plump, plushy furniture, the electric floor lamps
with their fringed shades, the heavy lace curtains at
the windows, the fireplace with the papery-looking
logs that burned gas when it was cold, the thick carpet
under her feet that felt almost like walking on grass
—everything was the same.

Then she stopped short, startled by what for a moment she took for two strangers. Then she saw that
they were herself and her father, reflected in the big
mirror above the fireplace. Her father's weather-beaten
face and sun-bleached hair looked all wrong against
the soft dimness of the room. But she—she was worse.
She was a gawky, bony child in a dress that was too
tight, faded to a dinginess made more pathetic by the
brighter strip at the bottom where the hem had been
let out, and by the fresh new patch below the shoulder.

Worse still was the sullen, sun-browned face, glaring defiantly from under a tangle of wind-blown, straw-colored hair.

It was terrible. She and her father looked like invaders, not visitors. Across the room, her father seated himself on the sofa. Perched stiffly on its edge, his calloused hands gripping each other tightly between his knees, he looked angry and uncomfortable. How could anyone look so different, Cindy wondered, without really changing at all. Her father was a fine-looking man, strong and self-assured. Yet, simply by coming into this place he had grown suddenly homely, awkward, and afraid.

Cindy sat down carefully in one of the plushy chairs. She felt herself sink deep into its softness, and wished she could sink all the way out of sight. Since she couldn't, she smoothed her dress and her hair, and forced her lips into a smile.

Grandpa Ellsworth said jovially, "Have a cigar, Dave!"

Cindy's father shook his head and mumbled thanks.

Her grandfather lit a cigar for himself, blew out a small puff of smoke and then a bigger one, settled back in his chair. "Hope you've been thinking about that opportunity I mentioned to you, Dave."

Dave Martin said gruffly, "I've thought about it."

"Well!" Grandpa Ellsworth beamed. "Running the Gem would put any man in a solid position. Put him where he's somebody in the neighborhood. Nice apartment goes with the job, too. Warm, comfortable, only a couple of blocks away from the theater. Whether you realize it or not, Dave, plenty of men would give their eyeteeth for a chance at it."

Cindy stared from her grandfather to her father and back again. Her jaw dropped with astonishment. Before she knew it, she had made a little gulping noise of dismay. Grandpa Ellsworth turned and looked at her. He seemed surprised to see her there.

"Well, Cindy! You don't want to sit moping in here, do you? You run out and find Marcella and David. They're in the back yard."

"I thought I was going to see my mother," Cindy protested.

"You will, later. She's resting now. You just go on out the side door there, and around to the back of the house. Now, run along."

Slowly, Cindy got up and went out. As she did, her alarm faded. Of course Grandpa had only been talking about his business, the way he always did. It had been silly to think he wanted her father to come and work in a theater, even sillier to think Dad would let himself be shut up in one place, doing the same job from one end of the year to the other.

Following the smooth cement sidewalk around the corner of the house, Cindy saw Marcy sitting primly, swinging herself gently back and forth on a broad seat suspended by two chains from a limb of a tall tree. Davy was playing in a big sandbox near by. He made a subdued roar of engine noises as he guided a toy truck up the side of a sand mountain. Beyond a stretch of smoothly clipped grass was a playhouse painted spotless white, with a red-shingled roof and green shutters at the windows.

She had stepped so softly over the grass that they hadn't heard her coming. They hadn't seen her, either. For a moment Cindy stood watching them, half choked by the happiness that swelled up inside her. The little ones had grown and changed, but they were still Marcy and Davy. Davy had been a baby, and now he was a small boy. Marcy was taller. Her tousled curls had grown longer, and had been trained into tidy cork-screws. But the change was more than that. Their faces were no longer browned by the sun, but freshly pink and white. Their hands and arms were smooth and clean, with no trace of scrapes, scratches, bruises or mosquito bites. Marcy wore a ruffly pink dress and shiny patent-leather sandals. Davy had on a sailor suit, white trimmed with blue braid. Against their background of smooth grass, shapely trees and bright paint, they reminded her of the make-believe children in the windows of the big department store. And the play yard was like one of the scenes, too clean and perfect to be real.

Cindy looked down at her scuffed brown oxfords, one ripped halfway down the side, the broken laces haphazardly knotted. She felt as out of place as a scare-crow dropped by mistake into one of those store windows. The next minute she felt even worse. Because suddenly Davy looked up and saw her.

His eyes, and then his mouth, opened wide. With a terrified wail, he ran to the swing and scrambled up beside Marcy. He seemed to be trying to squeeze himself small, so that he could hide behind her.

For a moment Marcy looked as frightened as Davy. Then she smiled, and reached out one hand toward Cindy while she patted Davy's shoulder comfortingly.

"Don't cry, Davy! It's Cindy. Our big sister, Cindy. Don't you remember how she used to tell us stories? About the Three Bears, and everything? Come on— say hello to Cindy."

Davy shook his head, trying to hide his face in Marcy's curls.

Marcy said comfortingly, "It's all right, Cindy. He didn't remember Mama, either, when she came from the hospital. He acted just the same way. But he got over it. Now he says he remembered her all the time. It's only because he's so little."

"I know," Cindy said. And of course it was true. Davy had been only a baby when he saw her last, and babies didn't remember things. But that didn't stop its hurting when she thought of the way he had looked at her and begun to cry.

"We came to take you home," Cindy said. "You and Mama and Davy."

Marcy shook her head. "We're not going. Didn't anybody tell you? You're going to come here. Dad's going to run one of Grandpa's theaters. We'll live in an apartment. But we can come here to play."

It was like an echo of what Grandpa had said, back there in the house. Her first guess had been right, after all. Still, she couldn't believe it.

"When you live here, you can go to the movies any

time," Marcy told her excitedly. "I go every day, almost. Hilda takes me."

"Is Hilda that woman who opened the door?" Cindy scowled. "I hate her."

"Oh, she's nice," Marcy insisted. "We get in to the movies for nothing. Grandpa gives us passes. Mary Pickford is my favorite. Don't you think I look like her, kind of? Hilda says I do. She fixes my curls like hers, even."

Marcy smoothed her skirt, and stretched out her white-stockinged legs so that the sun struck her sandals and made them gleam. "Don't you like my new clothes? Grandma bought them at Simonson's. That's the biggest store in town. When you're here, Grandma will buy you some. It's fun to go shopping. When I try things on all the clerks in Simonson's say, 'Isn't she a lovely little lady?'"

"Ladies aren't so stuck up!" Cindy said rudely.

Marcy looked hurt. "I didn't say I was lovely. That's what they say."

Cindy was silent, thinking about going into the big, beautiful department store and trying on new dresses, ready-made. Only—she looked down at her hands, brown and calloused, with the black under her fingernails that had resisted all her scrubbing, and all Dad's scraping with his penknife. The angry red cut along the side was just beginning to scab over. The people who sold the dresses would never call her a lovely little lady.

While they talked, Davy had stopped crying. At last he got down from the swing and went back to the sandbox. He began to play with his toy truck again, only once in a while glancing uneasily at Cindy.

Cindy looked at her little sister scornfully. "Movies and new clothes!" she said jeeringly. "What fun is that? I'll bet they don't let you out of the yard unless that old Hilda's got you by the hand. I can go to the woods any time I want to. And swimming, in the creek. I can do whatever I want, and help Dad with everything. We run things to suit ourselves, and I have lots of fun. We're not moving to town. Who wants to live in an apartment, where you probably can't even have a dog? Dad would have told me if we were going to do anything like that. Anyway, he wouldn't do it. He's a farmer."

Marcy smiled confidently. "There's no use arguing about it, Cindy. It's all settled. My goodness, Daddy doesn't have to be a farmer all his life. Grandma says he'd be quite pre—pre—"

"Do you mean presentable?" Cindy asked coldly.

"Yes, that's what she said. She said if he got the dirt out from under his fingernails and put on some decent clothes no one would need to be ashamed of him."

"Who's ashamed of him now?" Cindy demanded furiously. "You?"

"Well—well, of course I'm not. That's just what Grandma said."

Someone called, "Lucinda!" It was their grandmother, standing by the back door. Moving as slowly as she dared, Cindy went over to her. Grandma smiled and bent down, turning her cheek for Cindy to kiss.

But Cindy didn't move. She would not kiss her, not after the way she had talked about Dad.

After a moment Grandma straightened up. She said briskly, "Goodness me, Lucinda! You're as brown as a gypsy. It seems to me you're old enough to think about your appearance. When your mother was a girl she never went into the sun without a hat. And gloves, to keep her hands nice. One of these days you'll want to look like a lady, and then you'll wish you'd been more careful. But I suppose it's no use talking to you. Your mother wants to see you now. Here, at least comb your hair before you go in."

Cindy followed her, saying nothing. Ever since she could remember, her grandmother had been trying to make her into a ladylike little girl. Every birthday and every Christmas, she sent such things as necklaces, manicure sets, little kits for sewing or doing embroidery work. Cindy thanked her politely and then put the things away in her dresser drawer where they lay unused. She knew her grandmother was trying to please her with the gifts. She just couldn't understand that Cindy would rather have had a jackknife or a sled. And of course Cindy couldn't tell her. That would be ungrateful and rude.

In the blue-tiled bathroom, Cindy combed her hair with defiant carelessness. Then she followed silently down the hall to a closed door, and waited while her grandmother knocked.

12 : A Choice to Make

"Cindy? Come in, dear."

It had to be her mother's voice, and yet it didn't sound the same. It was lower and slower, lacking the breathless hurry, the excitement it used to have. Cindy turned the knob, went in and closed the door.

Her mother was reclining on a long couch, propped up by gaily colored pillows. Her arms were stretched out. Cindy ran into them and snuggled close. For a long moment she forgot everything but the wonder of warmth and softness. So many days she had yearned, so many nights she had dreamed, of having her mother's arms around her again. Now it had come true, and it was sweeter even than she had imagined it would be. She clung like a baby, head on her mother's shoulder, eyes tightly closed to keep back tears of happiness.

There was wetness against her cheek, her mother's tears. Her mother's hand smoothed her hair, stroked her cheek. Her mother's voice said again and again, "Cindy! Oh, Cindy!" And then, "It's been such a long time. Such a terribly long time."

But Cindy knew she was too big a girl to act like this. Gradually she pulled herself free. She sat on the edge of the couch holding one of her mother's hands.

At last she managed to look at her. She was paler,

but not so thin. There was a new quietness in her face, in all of her, that was strange. One smooth white hand, the one Cindy wasn't holding, lay relaxed at her side. Cindy had never noticed, back in the days before her mother went away, that her hands were never still. Only the strangeness of seeing that quiet hand now reminded her.

"Are you well now?" Cindy asked anxiously.

Her mother laughed softly. "Yes, darling. I'm fine now. All cured, the doctor says."

"Was it just awful, being sick?" Cindy remembered the throbbing head, the terrible burning feeling, when she had had the measles. Had her mother felt that way, and for a long time?

"The worst part was being away from you all. Even Daddy could only talk to me from across the room when he came to visit."

"You're coming home with us today. You are, aren't you?"

"Afraid not, darling," her mother said. "Not just now."

"Then when can you?"

"Don't pester her, Cindy. She doesn't know." Cindy started at her father's voice from behind her. She hadn't seen him, hadn't even realized he was there. But there he was, sitting stiffly in a chair in the corner. His face looked harder and sterner than ever.

"Dad?" Cindy didn't want to ask him, but now she had to. "Marcy says we're all coming to live in town. She says you're going to work for Grandpa. Are you?"

"No!" Dad spat out the word as if it had a bad

taste. "Seems everybody's making plans for me. Even Marcy. They all know what I'm going to do better than I know myself."

"David," Cindy's mother said in her new, quiet voice, "I suppose Papa did take too much for granted. But he's so enthusiastic about his plan, and so sure it would be the best for us all. You might even like the work, if you'd only try. Just think—a decent job for you, a comfortable living, nicer things for the children. And it would mean we could all be together right away. Please don't just be stubborn. Think of the rest of us."

"I am thinking of the rest of you. You think you could be satisfied to live on your father's charity? I don't think you could for long. And I couldn't for one minute."

"But you can't call it charity, it's a job!" Cindy's mother cried. "Papa needs someone to manage the Gem. Why shouldn't it be you?"

"Because I'm the last man in the world he'd hire, if I weren't married to you. It's not only that I don't know the first thing about how to run a theater. It's that I'd look as out of place there as a hog in church."

"But you could learn. You're smart. And I could help. This is something I know about. I could show you about keeping the books, and all sorts of things. I used to do it for Papa."

"Thanks." But Dad's voice sounded sarcastic instead of grateful. "You're right. I could learn how to do it. But I've already got the job I want. You said a decent job? Well, if you and your father think it's more decent to peddle movie tickets to people than it is to raise the bacon and eggs to feed them, I'll grant you the right to your opinion. But I don't have to agree with you. I want to do my own job, not one I have to take from your father and learn from you."

"Dave, you know I didn't mean it that way! Papa didn't, either. He loves us all, and wants to help. This job is the only thing he had to give, that he thought you might accept." Cindy's mother hid her face in one of the bright pillows.

Dad came over and patted her hair gently. "Don't get upset, Lucy. I'm sorry. I guess your father means well. But you ought to know I can't do it. We've got a home, our own place where we all belong. We've invested a good many hard years in our farm, and it's just getting ready to pay us back. Now you're well, it's time for you to come home."

Cindy's mother looked up. Her face was calm, and when she spoke her voice was quiet again. "I can't. Not now. Maybe in the spring. And—Dave, I think you should let Cindy stay here, too. She looks as if she's been working too hard, and it must be lonesome for her."

Dad said coldly, "She can stay if she wants to. It makes no difference to me."

"Wouldn't you like a nice vacation here with us, Cindy?" her mother coaxed.

Cindy looked from her mother to her father and then back again, in horrified disbelief. All this terrible time, her family had been torn apart because her mother was sick. Life had been uncomfortable, lonesome, stripped bare of good food, new clothes, family trips, money to spend, even church-going. When things had seemed too miserable to endure for another day she had gritted her teeth and reminded herself that it was only until her mother was well again. Then they would all be together, and things would be gay and hopeful the way they used to be. And now her mother was well. She had said so herself.

They could all be together now at home, but her mother wouldn't come home. They could all be together in town, but her father wouldn't stay. They must know they belonged together, that they had no right to be apart. Yet they insisted on staying apart, both of them.

If she stayed here they would all be together but one. There would be warmth and fun, and plenty of everything. She would have a fine school to go to, books from the library, movies, new clothes. After a while her hands would get as smooth and white as Marcy's, her hair as soft and tidy.

Then she thought of her father going home alone. Her father, who dreaded remembering his childhood, because then he had been alone. She thought of Mrs. Pickins pecking at the screen, the pigs running to the fence, Tom and Sade waiting for the apples she brought them every day. She thought of Ted, coming across the fields and looking for her.

She looked at her mother sternly. "I don't know why you think I'd want to stay here," she said. "Home is a lot better. I like having plenty to do. And it's not lonesome. It's fun. I'd rather go with Dad."

She kissed her mother good-bye, and without another word followed her father out the door.

13 : Homecoming

The ride back from Grandpa's house was like a bad dream. Cindy kept feeling that in a moment she would wake up and everything would be all right. And yet all along she knew that she was awake and that it was real.

Jouncing about on the hard seat, nearly deafened by the roar and rattle of going too fast over the bumpy roads, she had no feeling of going home. She was all aching emptiness inside, as if her heart and stomach and all the rest had been whisked away like a loose tooth.

Beside her, her father crouched tensely over the wheel. It frightened her to look at his face. Its grim, angry lines seemed set hard as stone, so that it was impossible to imagine that he would ever smile again.

They rode on and on. The hollow ache became more insistent and more painful. At last she realized that part of the pain was hunger. She hadn't eaten since that hurried breakfast, so long ago she could hardly remember it. They had planned for dinner at Grandpa's, but she hadn't cared about food after the disappointment of learning that her mother wasn't coming home with them.

She had wanted only to get away from everyone, to be alone with her sadness and her resentment. Her father had felt the same way, she knew. She remembered his mumbled excuses, his uneasy hurry to be away.

She remembered the forced cheerfulness of her grandparents' voices, and the worried looks they couldn't quite hide. "But surely you can stay long enough to eat something," her grandmother had coaxed. "Lucinda, dear, won't you change your mind and stay with us for a while? We'll have a chance to shop for clothes, and have all kinds of fun. Please?"

When she and her father had still insisted on leaving, Grandpa had said heartily. "Now, don't worry, Dave. We'll take good care of Lucy. See you again soon."

But all the cheerful words had meant nothing at all. They couldn't change the fact that the magic day, the day she and her father had waited for so long, had come at last. And still, they were going home alone.

The ride ended at last. Trying to sound cheerful, Cindy said, "Well, here we are."

Her father didn't seem to hear her. Without looking at her, he got out of the truck and walked into the house. By the time she had changed her clothes and come downstairs he had disappeared. Even if she had known where he was, she wouldn't have dared follow him.

By this time she felt faint and dizzy with hunger. She rummaged forlornly through the cupboards for something to eat, anything. There was nothing but a piece of cold sausage, stuck in a puddle of congealed grease, a couple of boiled potatoes, and some bread. There was no fire in the stove, and she dared not disobey her father's orders and start one. Milk and butter were in the cellar, but she just couldn't face its dark shadows. She forced down the dry bread and potatoes and the sausage somehow, though they kept sticking in her throat. When she had finished, the hollow ache was still there, but with a cold, heavy lump in the middle of it.

The slanting light through the screen door reminded her it was time for evening chores. No matter what happened, those had to be done. So she started.

Just as always, the chickens came running to the sound of the pump, crowding around her feet with eager, welcoming sounds. The pigs raced to her whistle, jostling each other for the best places around the trough and squealing with anticipation. The cows hurried through the barn door and into their stanchions. The white cats ran from all directions, shoving one another aside in their haste to rub themselves against Cindy's legs. Every creature was wildly glad to see her. They all needed her.

But if she had stayed in town Dad would have fed them, of course. They wouldn't have missed her for long.

She ran down the lane, with Shep barking and frisking around her. On her way through the orchard she paused long enough to pick up a few apples from the windfalls that covered the ground. Then she ran on, along the edge of the newly planted wheat field, to the corner of the pasture.

Tom and Sade were near the middle of the field, grazing side by side. Cindy whistled, and their heads came up. Their ears pointed alertly toward her, and they began to walk in her direction. Tom was in front, as always. Sade followed close behind. They moved slowly, but there was eagerness in the way their ears strained forward, the way they lifted their feet lightly through the brownish grass. With each step grasshoppers flew up in quick flurries, like water splashing from a puddle.

Cindy gave them each an apple, and they munched contentedly. Tom swallowed his first, stretched his head across the top of the fence and nipped gently at the edge of her pocket. She took out another apple and held it balanced on her palm. Tom picked it up daintily between his teeth, rolled it carefully into his mouth, and crunched it slowly with a look of perfect contentment. Sade, too, thrust forward her head.

Cindy said, "That's all, Sade. No more." Probably she should have brought four, she thought. But Tom did seem to find a special joy in having more than his share. And Tom was such a dear.

Leaning her head against the firm smoothness of Tom's neck, Cindy scratched him gently just below the ear, where he most liked to be scratched. His coat felt like satin against her cheek, but better than satin because it was alive and warm. He smelled nice, too, with a special clean, sharp scent that was like nothing else except horse.

The sun was warm on her back. The monotonous buzz and whir of insect life all round her, the rattle of the dry stubble stirred by the breeze, made her feel drowsy and comfortable. Time drifted by.

Then Tom made a soft little snorting noise, and shifted his weight a bit to the left. Cindy heard the swish of Sade's long tail, and the impatient stamp of one of her hoofs. She realized that she had been leaning against Tom for a long time, and that he had been standing as patiently still as a statue. Poor Tom, the flies must have been tormenting him. She stepped back, and patted his side apologetically.

Now Cindy could see the other horses heading for the barnyard. Along the winding path to the pasture they moved slowly, in single file, switching their tails constantly against the flies. Now and then they paused to nip a mouthful of grass. Queenie came first, leading the way as always. Then Stormy, in a flurry of pauses, sudden side excursions and quick dashes. Then Inky and Sooty, then Captain, and finally Jerry.

"You must want a drink, too. Go on!" Cindy gave Tom a little shove. He blinked at her lazily, then turned his head to look at the other horses. At last he nudged Sade with his nose, turned and moved slowly away. Sade followed placidly, her steps in time with his.

Now lonesomeness descended on Cindy like an actual pain. There was no comfort in any of these creatures. Of course they were only animals, and couldn't know how much she needed it. They couldn't speak, even if they could have understood.

But her father could understand, he could speak. If only he'd said, "Thanks for coming along, Cindy. I needed you." If only he'd even looked a little glad. But he didn't seem to care at all.

A piercing whistle sounded from the direction of the house. Cindy lifted her head to listen. That was their secret signal, hers and Ted's. They had used it to call to each other ever since the time, years and years ago, when Ted had first learned to whistle and then taught her. It had been a long time since Ted had used it.

Cindy put her fingers to her mouth and whistled between them, loud and shrill. She waited. In a moment there was the sound of running footsteps, and then Ted's voice, calling, "Cindy! Where are you?"

"Right here. Over by the pasture fence." She walked toward him slowly, and they met at the edge of the orchard. Ted was frowning anxiously.

"Mom cooked up an extra pot of chicken and noodles, and baked a couple of extra pies. Said she wasn't having your mother start cooking the minute she came home, and your father could growl as much as he wanted to. We were watching all afternoon, but when the truck went by she wasn't in it. So we decided your grandfather was driving her in his car, later. Mom sent me up to find out. Afraid we might have missed seeing them go by, somehow."

Cindy shook her head. "She's not coming," she mumbled.

"She's not? I guess I must have read your note wrong. I thought you said it was today she was coming. Mom's going to be disappointed. She was so thrilled, you'd have thought somebody was sending her a million dollars. When is she coming?"

"I don't know," said Cindy, "maybe never."

"Never? You're kidding. What do you want to say a thing like that for?"

"Because it's true. She won't say when. She says maybe in the spring. Spring comes, maybe it'll be something else. She wants us to come and live in town. Of course Dad wouldn't ever do that."

"Why not?" Ted asked matter-of-factly. "If it was really better for your mother, I should think he'd want to."

There in town, it had seemed plain as day that her father was right, that this was where he had to stay. Now Ted's simple question made the good reasons seem unimportant. To cover her uncertainty she said angrily, "Don't be silly! He just couldn't."

Ted looked at her thoughtfully for a moment and then said, "Well, then she'll come here. It won't be long. I expect maybe she doesn't feel quite as well as she says. She has to be pretty strong to start taking care of that house and the little kids. Maybe she'd be able to look after one of those little apartments in town, with everything handy. But it would be different out here. Your house is nice and all that, but my mother says it's a woman-killer. The kind they used to build when help was cheap. It's cold and drafty in the winter, too. You don't notice it, maybe, because you're used to it. But your mother would."

Cindy shook her head stubbornly. "Dad's told her how we've been doing everything in the house. We could do all the work. She'd only have to rest, and keep herself warm."

"Don't worry, Cindy," Ted said comfortingly. "She'll come as soon as she can. She wants to be with you."

Cindy's face brightened a bit. "Say, that's right! She wanted me to stay at Grandpa's with her."

"That would be fun!" Ted exclaimed. "Didn't you want to?"

"Of course I did," Cindy admitted. "Who wouldn't? Oh, it's so lovely there. So neat and warm, and everything new. Everything you could dream about to eat. Marcy says she goes to the movies nearly every day. And Grandma said she'd get me lots of new clothes."

"Boy, that would be all right!" Ted said enviously. "Wish somebody would invite me. Why in the world didn't you stay?"

Cindy turned away, blinking hard to hold back the tears that stung her eyes. "How could I? Dad and I both work as hard as we can, and still we never get as much done as we should. I couldn't have fun if I had to think about him here all by himself."

Ted frowned, looked as if he were ready to say something and then didn't. They started walking slowly toward the house. At last Ted said, "I guess I know how you feel. But it's funny. I ought to feel sorry for you, but really I envy you. Not that I'd ever want my family to have a lot of trouble like yours. But—it must feel good to know you're that important to anyone. Around our place there's nothing I can do that somebody else can't do better. Sometimes I think I could go away and nobody would know the difference."

"Of course they would," Cindy said softly. "I would, too." She wished she could find the right words to thank

Ted for what he had said. He had straightened out her tangled thoughts and made her know that it was right for her to be here. All at once the aching sadness, the doubts and the loneliness were all gone. She was her old strong self again, content to be where she belonged.

14 : A Break in the Weather

When that eventful Sunday was over it was hard to believe it had ever happened. Things went on much as before, with school and chores and the bleak discomfort of living in a house that seemed always chilled with emptiness.

The only thing that had changed was Cindy herself. First she told her father she was tired of drying dishes, and would rather wash for a change. This wasn't true. She hated washing dishes as much as she ever had. What she liked was the way the warm, soapy water soaked the stubborn dirt from under her nails, and softened the callouses on her hands. She remembered a half-empty bottle of the glycerine and rose water her mother used to put on her hands, looked for it, and at last found it in behind a stack of plates in the cupboard. Whenever she dried her hands she would smooth some on, delighting in its silky feeling and the way its scent clung around her.

She began to spend more time combing her hair, pushing it into waves and curling it around her finger as Mrs. Nichols had showed her. She experimented with different styles, trying out first the barrettes Mrs. Nichols had given her, then ribbons of different colors.

All this she did secretly at first, stealing moments

when her father wasn't around. She felt strangely ashamed, and would have been ready to retreat into her old carelessness if anyone had laughed, or remarked on the change.

But, as no one did, she grew bolder. She began to iron the jeans and shirts she wore around home. She even hunted out the necklaces and pins her grandmother had given her over the years and tried wearing first one and then the other to school. To her surprise, no one laughed. A couple of the girls even used them as an excuse to begin a conversation which Cindy found herself enjoying.

But if her father noticed any change, he made no comment. He went about his work, speaking more rarely than ever and smiling not at all. If his steps fell a bit more slowly than they used to and his shoulders drooped a trifle, the difference was so small that anyone but Cindy would scarcely have noticed it. He and Cindy never talked of the Sunday in town.

But Cindy and Ted talked about it sometimes. He came over nearly every day to help her with her chores. They talked and argued about all sorts of things as they worked—school, books they had read, the stars, airplanes, what the world would be like by the time they were as old as their parents. But whatever they began by talking about, always they returned to the puzzle of Cindy's mother. Her letters were cheerful and loving, but they said nothing about coming home. Ted and Cindy went over and over everything that had happened, wishing there were something they could do to put things right. But they found no answer.

On a Tuesday in October a strange, breathless heat settled down and didn't lift even after darkness came. On Wednesday morning the animals were oddly restless and quarrelsome. The hens puffed out their feathers and screeched at one another threateningly over their food, instead of crooning contentedly as they usually did. Shep snarled at Daisy, the young Jersey cow, when she hesitated too long before going through the cow-barn door, and Daisy lowered her head and rushed at Shep menacingly. Even mild, long-suffering Sade squealed in irritable protest when Tom snatched a mouthful of hay from her manger, and lunged in his direction with teeth bared and ears laid back. Cindy finished her chores, sweaty and out of temper.

It was in the early afternoon that the wind came. School had just taken up after lunch, and Cindy was bent over her desk, absorbed in arithmetic. She must have missed the beginning of it, because when she noticed the rushing, rattling sound and looked up all the other boys and girls, even Miss Emery, had stopped their work and were staring out the windows. Outside, the air was full of dust and leaves and sticks, flying almost straight across her field of vision. Trees bent, and as she watched one snapped and fell with a crash across the graveled driveway.

"It's all right," Miss Emery said sharply. "Only a little windstorm. Back to work, now."

The seventh-grade half of the class was supposed to be reciting in history, while the eighth grade studied. But neither of them was getting much done. They all kept glancing up to watch what was going on outside.

They soon saw that it wasn't going to be a tornado. It was just a windstorm, no worse than storms they had all seen before. Still, it was exciting.

It kept getting darker until Miss Emery had to turn on the electric lights. But they had been on scarcely five minutes when they flickered and went out, and then it seemed twice as dark as before. No one could see the things written on the blackboard.

Miss Emery snapped the switch a couple of times and then sighed. "I suppose the wind must have blown the wires down."

So they chose up sides and had a spelling bee, which Cindy won after an exciting battle with Jimmy Sands, the banker's son. Then they sang some songs, and at last it was time to go home.

The school bus had parked in the street because of the fallen tree, and the boys and girls were forced to scramble up a steep bank and squeeze against a fence to get to it. As they got in, fine drops of rain were blowing out of the northeast. Cindy gasped at the stinging cold against her cheeks, and shivered at the way the drops rattled against the windows of the bus. As they drove up the main street there were craned necks and excited cries. The wooden sign that had hung outside the pool room had blown from its support and been hurled across the street, right through the big window in the front of the hardware store. Men were scurrying about with boards and ladders, trying to rig up some way of keeping the wind and rain from doing more damage inside. They were shouting to one another, and as the bus passed Cindy heard a great burst of laughter.

That was strange, Cindy thought. Two of the men were the elderly brothers who owned the store. They couldn't be happy about having their window smashed and part of their stock wet and blown about. They must be feeling the same way she did, frightened and dismayed at the damage the storm had done and still might do, yet not able to keep from being thrilled with the excitement of it.

When she reached home, with the rain coming down harder than ever, her father seemed to have caught the same feeling. As she helped him get the livestock inside, close doors and windows and secure everything they could against the weather, he moved and talked swiftly. His face and eyes were alive again, full of energy and excitement.

Ted didn't appear that evening as usual, but Cindy hardly missed him. It was natural that in weather like this he'd be busy at home.

Next morning the wind had died, but the rain went on. It came down harder and harder. In the afternoon the school bus splashed through deep puddles in the road. Cindy and her father sloshed ankle-deep in mud, feeding the livestock. They were quiet and gloomy. Where yesterday's wind and driving rain had been an exciting challenge, this monotonous downpour was only a dull misery.

"We needed rain all right," Cindy's father said. "But this is too much of a good thing. If it keeps up, people will have to start getting out of the bottoms."

"I'm glad we don't live there." Cindy thanked her lucky stars that wishes didn't always come true. She had often longed for one of the rich, bottom-land farms next to the river, like the one where Ted's family lived. There the deep, black soil held its moisture even in dry seasons, and yielded bumper crops. Through normal seasons the levees, high banks of earth along the edges of the stream, held the water to its course. But when too much rain came at once, tremendous pressures were built up. If they lived in the bottoms now, she and her father would be dreading the break in the levee that could mean the loss of everything they had, maybe even their lives. She wondered what Ted was doing, whether he was as scared as she would have been in his place.

Next day, Friday, there was no traffic on the road. Even the school bus didn't appear. That meant that somewhere there was water over the road too deep for passage. The day dragged by, with nothing to do except chores; Cindy spent most of it reading and looking out the windows at the rain.

Saturday it still rained. Cindy helped her father do some listless dusting and sweeping and picking up. When they had finished he said, "I think I'll see how things are over at the Nichols' place. With so much rain, they're bound to need some help."

"I can help, too." Cindy reached for her jacket.

Her father shook his head. "I don't want you anywhere near that river. You look after things here." Then he saddled Captain and rode off.

Cindy settled down with a book, but today she couldn't lose herself in the story. She kept seeing horrible pictures in her mind, of the great earthen banks giving way, of torrents of muddy water surging through, of her father being swept away and lost forever. Then, of Ted being swept away and lost forever. She hoped he was watching out for himself, not getting into any danger.

The day dragged by as if it would never end. Cindy welcomed the evening chores, and made them last as long as she could. Still there was no sign of her father. It seemed as if she had been alone in the chill, rain-soaked gloom for a dismal eternity.

Her father's return, after dark, made Cindy feel weak with relief. He reported that the levees were holding. It had seemed safe for most of the men who had come to help to go home for the night.

"Are—are the Nicholses all right?" Cindy asked.

"Sure!" Her father rumpled her hair playfully. "Ted's having the time of his life."

Sunday it still rained. With her father gone again to help at the levees, Cindy spent most of the morning with the animals. They were growing restless in their confinement, and so was she.

At last she returned to the house and settled down to read. She wished she had a new, exciting book that would make her forget the storm and the worries that came with it. Then she was startled to hear a loud knocking at the door.

It was Ted, in high boots and a raincoat, carrying a big basket. Behind him, more surprisingly, was his mother. She was similarly dressed, and carried a large package wrapped in oilcloth. They took off their wet boots and coats on the porch and came into the kitchen.

Cindy ran to fetch towels to wipe the water from their faces. They put down their packages and sank into chairs, gasping for breath.

"Well, Cindy!" Mrs. Nichols panted. "Think you can put us up for a while? They made us get out. Said it was no place for a woman. And Ted was elected to come along and look after us."

Ted scowled. "Fifteen years old, and pretty near as big as any of 'em, and they're treating me like a kid. I've got you here safe. Now I'm going back there and help."

"You're doing no such thing," Mrs. Nichols told him firmly. "You just settle yourself right here out of harm's way, until this is over."

"No, Mom." Ted's voice shook a little, but his blue eyes were determined. "I've always minded what you told me before, but this is different. I've got to go back."

Mrs. Nichols' lips quivered. Tears welled up in her eyes. But she said nothing more. Ted walked quickly to the door and through it.

Cindy caught up with him just outside. She clutched his arm and was surprised at its strength. Ted seemed suddenly taller, towering over her as he had never done before.

"Oh, please, Ted. Don't go. I'm so—so scared. Your mother is, too, can't you see it? Please don't leave us here all alone."

Ted looked down at her, surprised. For a moment the determination in his eyes seemed to soften. Then he shook his head. "You'll be all right," he told her.

"You're on high ground here. Nothing can happen. Can't you see I've got to go back?"

Reluctantly, Cindy nodded. She could understand. Ted was choosing the difficult way when he might have taken the easy. Maybe this was the first chance in his whole life to feel needed. "Please be careful," she whispered.

"Don't worry. I will." He touched her cheek gently with his wet, cold hand, and then was down the steps and gone, hidden behind the gray curtain of rain.

Cindy went back inside. Mrs. Nichols was stirring up the fire vigorously with the poker. "Well," she said with determined cheerfulness, "I'll make us something hot to drink, and you see what's in the basket. I brought along a few groceries, figuring you might not be fixed for company."

There was cold fried chicken in the basket, home-made bread, a jar of pickles, a huge bowl of Mrs. Nichols' famous potato salad, a couple of pies, a bag of coffee and another of sugar, a tin of cocoa. Cindy got milk and butter from the cellar, and set the table for two.

When they were settled she looked sheepishly across the table at Ted's mother. "I don't know what got into me out there," she admitted. "I begged him to stay. Told him I was—I was scared. And I know there's nothing to be afraid of here. Anyway, I never in my life admitted I was scared, even when I was. What will Ted think of me? I feel like a fool."

Mrs. Nichols chuckled. "Cindy, Ted's going to think twice as much of you as he ever did before. For this day he's feeling like a man, because there's something hard and dangerous for him to do. I couldn't see it at first. I've treated him as a child because—well, I guess I've always wanted to keep my youngest one a child. I did wrong, and you did right. You treated him as a strong man able to face things only a strong man can face. I didn't know you had it in you, Cindy. And you were frightened, really, weren't you? Admit it, now."

Cindy nodded shamefacedly. "But only that something might happen to Ted."

"With God's help nothing will," Mrs. Nichols said. "Not to Ted nor to any of them. We can only wait here and believe that. And have things ready to warm and feed them, or to take care of anybody that gets hurt."

"It's funny," Cindy said as she started to help Mrs. Nichols clear the table. "The other day Dad and I were talking about you, and the other people who live on bottom land. We were saying how awful that you might lose your crops and your buildings if things got bad. Now all we're wishing for is that nobody gets hurt or— or—"

"Or killed," Mrs. Nichols finished firmly. "Yes. There's nothing like real trouble to make folks remember what's important. Even me. Notice that package I brought along? My treasures. Deeds, a little money, my silverware, a few trinkets my grandmother passed down to me, family pictures. But I'd have thrown them away without thinking twice if they stood in the way of saving Ted's life, or mine. Or even a perfect stranger's, if it came to that.

"Anyway, suppose every crop was ruined? Every

building, every bit of livestock swept away? It would be bad, but not as bad as it sounds."

"How do you mean?" Cindy asked.

"You're not old enough to remember the last flood, are you? That was—why, I believe it was the year you were born. We were lucky, but a couple of families got washed out, a few miles down the river. Everybody pitched in to give them another start."

"Really? How does that work?" asked Cindy.

"Same as when somebody gets burned out, or hit with a tornado. All their neighbors and relatives throw in whatever they can spare. One might give lumber. Somebody else has furniture to spare. Other people chip in with food, seed, livestock, even money to keep things going. Then everybody pitches in to work, doing whatever he's best at. Building, painting, butchering, canning, sewing—gets to be kind of like a party before it's done."

"But don't the people mind? Taking—well, charity from their neighbors?"

"Of course not! Not when they've been hit by one of those big things they call an Act of God, a thing too big for anyone to handle by himself. They've helped out others before, and they know they will again. I'm surprised your father hasn't told you all about it. He's always one of the first to be there when there's need, doing what he can."

"Dad never did like to do much talking," Cindy said.

Mrs. Nichols sighed and shook her head. "Maybe it's not so much that he doesn't like to talk as that he never learned how."

Cindy stared at the big woman, puzzled and resentful.

Noticing her expression, Mrs. Nichols went on. "Now, don't think I'm saying he's stupid, or anything like that. He knows plenty of words, and he could put them together perfectly well. I suppose he just never got any practice."

"He and Mama used to talk together a lot," Cindy remembered.

"Yes, I suppose they did," Mrs. Nichols said. She fell silent, and when she spoke again it was on a new subject.

Cindy had never stayed up so late in her life as she did that night. She kept expecting Mrs. Nichols to send her to bed, and planning the arguments she would use to postpone a little longer her exile to the lonesome upstairs where there would be no sound except the steady pounding of the rain.

But Mrs. Nichols seemed to have forgotten the time. She kept on working, cleaning out cupboards, dusting and scrubbing and polishing. Cindy helped as much as she could, but it seemed she hardly knew how to do anything. Mrs. Nichols had to keep giving her directions, and in between she talked about many other things, but mostly about the time when she had been a girl. Cindy listened with interest, and in return related experiences and thoughts of her own.

But at last she began to get sleepy, and then sleepier and sleepier. The room blurred before her eyes, and Mrs. Nichols' words were only a meaningless buzzing in her ears.

Waking to a feeling of cramped discomfort, heat on

her face, a confusion of noises in her ears, Cindy had a moment of alarm. She kept her eyes closed tight, knowing she wasn't in her familiar room. Where was she, and how had she come here?

She opened her eyes, and saw that she was on the couch in the living room. Sun slanting through the window had been striking directly at her cheek and into her eyes. Slowly the memory of last night returned to her mind, and she realized that she must have fallen into a sort of walking sleep and been brought here by Mrs. Nichols.

But then, when she had fallen asleep that had left Mrs. Nichols alone in the house. Now there were several voices, mingling with a clatter of dishes. And there was sunshine. Then it all clicked together in her drowsy mind, and she was suddenly wide awake. The storm was over. While she slept, the danger had passed.

Cindy sat up, rubbed her eyes, smoothed her hair, put on her shoes. She opened the kitchen door quietly and looked in. Mrs. Nichols was pouring coffee into one of the thick white cups on the table. Around the table half a dozen men were sitting—her father, Mr. Nichols, Ted's older brothers, Bob and Jim, a couple of others whose names she didn't remember. For a moment she was chilled with panic because Ted wasn't there. But then the satisfaction on the tired, grimy faces of the men told her that he, and everyone, had come through all right.

After a moment her father saw her and said, "Come on in, Cindy. The levees held. Everything's all right."

"Sure enough," Mr. Nichols affirmed with a smile.

"We beat the old river again. Rain stopped hours ago. Water's already going down. Thank God for good neighbors. It took all every one of us could do to keep things under control."

While they ate and drank, the men talked over the days just past. Now that the effort and danger were over, they could belittle their labors and laugh at the risks they had taken. Since Cindy took for granted her father's strength and courage, she accepted without surprise his part in the most hair-raising moments. But at the men's casually including Ted as one of themselves she was filled with such a glow of happiness and pride that she had to turn away, pretending to gaze out the window for fear her face would betray her unusual interest in him.

An hour later they were all gone. The comradeship of the emergency was over, and each family would face the task of cleaning up, repairing damage, returning everything to normal. Cindy put on jacket and boots, and followed her father outside.

The sun was shining on seas of mud and dozens of glistening puddles. Though it was Monday, there would be no school. There hadn't been time for the standing water to dry up or drain away. But it was a beautiful day. If only Ted had come over, even for a moment, things would have been perfect. But Cindy firmly put away that thought, reminding herself of all the work there must be to do at the Nichols' place.

She raced through her chores. It was fun to open the doors and let the animals out into the clean, sunny air. Though the chickens shared with the horses a distaste for mud, and picked their way fastidiously to the driest spots, it was plain that they, too, felt the joy of freedom.

As she stood watching Tom and Sade walk down the lane, staying to the solid ground close to the fence, Cindy felt something touch her head. It was her father's hand, gently smoothing her hair. She looked up at him, smiling. After being gloomy and silent for so long, her father seemed to be telling her now that he was glad she had chosen to be here with him.

For what seemed like a long time he looked down at her, an expression of gentle sadness on his weather-beaten face. At last he said huskily, "Let's take a walk, Cindy."

They went out through the feed lot and down the lane. Their boots squished loudly in the sticky mud, which clung stubbornly to the rubber, building up until Cindy's feet were almost too heavy to lift. Whenever they came to a puddle she waded through it to let the water wash her boots clean.

"Potatoes ought to be all right," Dad said thoughtfully. "Provided it doesn't set in to rain again. We had most of them out, anyway."

They skirted the wheat field. "No harm done," her father decided. "Might be some seed washed out along the slope. But there's time to replant."

The pasture, which had been scorched brown by the drought, already showed greener. The storm had brought it new life. It seemed that the frightening weather had been a blessing, after all.

But her father was no more cheerful. In a few minutes Cindy understood why. She had forgotten the corn.

Now the field stretched in front of her, and to both sides as far as she could see. Where there had been long rows of ripening stalks, stunted from drought it was true and thinly set with ears, now there was only ruin. The stalks lay bent, twisted, tangled in a flattened mass. Walking beside her father as he picked his way into the field, she saw the ears flattened against the mud, some half buried in it.

Her father's face was set, its lines cut deep. He looked much as he had on that ride home from the city, only older and more tired.

They turned back toward the house, walking slowly side by side. In unconscious imitation of her father, Cindy slouched along with her head bent forward, her hands deep in the pockets of her overalls.

"It wouldn't have been much of a crop at best," her father said. "Anybody could tell this wasn't going to be a corn year. Too wet and cold at the beginning of the season. Too dry later on. But I was counting on enough for feed and a couple of hundred dollars' worth to sell. That would have been enough."

Cindy tried to offer consolation. "We can turn the hogs in on it. They'll dig it out. Ought to fatten them up good."

Her father nodded. "That's right. We'll do that. But it takes time to make fat hogs."

Cindy remembered the man at the bank, and what he had said about the notes. The thirty days weren't up yet, but they would be, long before the half-grown shoats had become fat hogs. Cindy's mind flew in desperation from one end of the farm to the other, searching for something that would bring in the money they needed. With sickening certainty, she knew there was only one thing.

They had nearly reached the barn before she found her voice. She said huskily, "Guess we're lucky Ben Thompson took such a fancy to Tom."

Dad touched her shoulder briefly and nodded. "Guess we are, at that."

They didn't talk about it any more. There was no more to say. For the rest of the day Cindy took every chance to look at Tom, to touch him, to feed him. She felt she had to notice and remember everything about him, all the tiny things she had never paid attention to before because she thought he would always be there. She yearned over details like the finely ridged blackness of his hoofs, the delicate curve of his ears.

When the rest of the horses went to pasture, Cindy shut Tom and Sade in the barn. After all the chores were done, she groomed Tom with painstaking care. Once she heard Dad come to the door, and knew he was watching her. She pretended she didn't know he was there, and at last he went away without speaking. She went on brushing and brushing Tom's coat, combing every snarl from his mane and tail. Finally there was no more to do, and besides it was too dark to see.

Carefully she put away the currycomb and the brush. Then came back and stood beside Tom. It was too dark to see even his whiteness, but she could feel his warm, solid presence beside her. She could hear his breathing, calm and contented, unaware of what would happen tomorrow.

Burying her face in the smooth warm hollow of his shoulder, Cindy surrendered herself to despair. She was too old and too big to cry, but tonight she didn't care. Sobs tore through her. Tears streamed down her face. They soaked the silky hair of Tom's coat.

She cried for a long time, at first stormily, then more quietly. The tears kept on and on, as if every one she had ever forced back had been waiting to pour itself out, now that the way was clear.

15 : A Broken Team

Next evening Cindy sped through her evening chores with tense, cold efficiency. She didn't waste time talking to any of the animals. Though Goliath stuck his snout inquiringly between the boards of the fence, she didn't scratch behind his ear. Neither did she pause to stroke any of the white cats. Even Shep, though he wagged his whole body in an ecstasy of friendliness, could get nothing from her but a brusque, "Down, sir!" and a rather skimpy panful of milk.

Cindy opened the stable door. It was empty except for Sade. At the creak of the hinges, Sade's head flung up. Her loud neigh, piercingly shrill, made Cindy shrink back for a moment. Then she walked determinedly forward and began to fill Sade's manger with hay. She did it without looking at the mare, but it was impossible not to hear the low, questioning whicker, then the loud sighing, letting out of breath, then the silence. Cindy didn't touch Sade. She didn't speak to her. She filled the manger quickly, and left without having let her eyes stray to Tom's empty stall.

Outside, she met her father. "Haven't you forgotten something?" he asked her quietly.

She shook her head. "I don't think so."

"You forgot to take Sade out for water. It's your job to look after her until she gets used to managing for herself."

"All right." Cindy went back and untied Sade's halter rope. She led her out, waited for her to drink, then led her back. She did it resentfully, scornful of Sade's hesitations and tremblings. She clenched her teeth in annoyance when Sade hung back to neigh loudly again and again, bracing herself stubbornly against Cindy's impatient tugs. With head high and ears strained forward, Sade neighed, and then listened with quivering eagerness a dozen times, before at last she let herself be led in.

Cindy had always scorned Sade for her clumsiness and her timidity. Now, she decided, she hated her. Sade was ugly and stupid, too stupid to know she might as well stop crying over what couldn't be helped and start learning how to fend for herself. Cindy glared at Sade angrily as she tied the halter rope. She had no right to be here, now that Tom was gone.

At supper, Cindy picked listlessly at the cabbage and potatoes her father had boiled with a piece of fat pork. Her father watched her anxiously.

At last he said, "Eat your supper, Cindy. No use sitting there with a long face."

She sighed. "I know." She ate a few bites. Then she said, "I was thinking about poor Tom. What do you suppose he's doing now?"

Her father scowled. "Tom's all right. Ben Thompson's got a better stable than ours. And he won't be short of feed this winter the way we will."

"Yes, but—" Cindy gave her father an appealing look. "He'll miss Sade."

Her father gave a grating laugh. "Miss Sade? Why should he? What's she ever done for him, except see that he had less fun and more work?"

"But they've always been together," Cindy protested.

"The old rascal's probably tickled to death to be rid of her. And I don't blame him, either. Don't you fool away your time feeling sorry for Tom. He's smart enough to know when he's well off."

Cindy nodded reluctant agreement. But she didn't feel happier. She felt worse. And she saw that her father didn't look happy either.

"No use being soft-hearted fools," he went on harshly. "Everybody has to look out for himself in this world. Animals or people, it's all the same. Nobody turns down a soft life for a hard one. Nobody's got a right to expect anybody else to. A person would have to be blind not to see that."

"I guess so," Cindy admitted. She shivered at the thought of Sade, calling and calling for Tom, hoping and hoping for him to come back. She was only a horse, so she couldn't understand that Tom was happier without her. Still, she would have to realize some day that he wasn't going to come back. Even though she was blind, she couldn't help seeing that.

Caring for Sade meant getting up a little earlier in the morning, hurrying a little faster, finishing a little later at night. The first thing she did was to lead Sade out and stake her where there was plenty of grass. Then, the last thing before she left for school or went in for the night, she watered her and tied her in her stall.

Sade went on being helpless and frightened. When Cindy led her out she followed with fear and trembling. She accepted food or water with grudging suspicion, and every few moments raised her head to sniff the air and neigh, sometimes loudly, sometimes softly and questioningly.

Cindy began by resenting the job and despising Sade. But it was impossible to spend so much time with any animal in coldness and silence. Little by little, Cindy found herself talking to Sade.

"Good girl!" she would say gently. "It's all right. Cindy won't let anything hurt you. Easy now, you're doing fine."

Little by little, she found herself patting and stroking Sade, touching her reassuringly when she began to tremble. Very gradually, so that Cindy didn't even know what was happening until it had already become a fact, she found that she didn't despise Sade any more.

She found herself thinking that Sade was the one she should have liked best all along, not Tom. She wondered how she could have failed to see all the good in Sade. There was her patient industry, steadily doing Tom's share of the work while he took every opportunity to shirk. There was her lack of resentment at Tom's thieving. Cindy was ashamed that she had once thought Sade's meekness was due to stupidity. She saw now that it was the only way Sade had known how to express her love for Tom, and her gratitude for the things he did for her.

A week went by. Each day Cindy watched for a change in Sade. Soon she would give up watching, listening, waiting for Tom, and begin to forget. Only then would she begin to learn independence and contentment. But when a change did come, it was not the one Cindy had been waiting for.

When Ted appeared for the first time since the storm, it was to find Cindy washing dried blood from Sade's face with a cloth dipped in warm water. He whistled with pity and astonishment.

"What happened?" he demanded. "I thought your old Tom always looked after her to see she didn't hurt herself."

"He did," Cindy said tightly. "But he's gone. Dad sold him. Didn't you know?"

Ted shook his head. "We've been so busy over at our place, I guess we haven't heard much of anything since the storm. Fixing fences, shoring up the corncrib where the foundation just about washed out from under one side, and I don't know what all. This is the first chance I've had to get away. Who'd your father sell him to? Ben Thompson? Thought you said he'd turned him down."

"He did. Said he'd never break up the team."

"Well, then, why did he?" Ted asked.

"Whoa, girl," Cindy murmured, as Sade winced away from her attempt to clean the deepest of the cuts. She glared at Ted, for the moment almost hating him. How could he understand, with the Nichols family so prosperous and untroubled?

"M-o-n-e-y, money," she said scathingly. "We could

have managed if it hadn't been for the storm. With the corn ruined, it was the only way to pay what we owed."

"I'm sorry," Ted said. "Up on high ground the way you are, I never thought you'd be hurt."

Cindy smiled wryly. "I guess we didn't have anywhere near the damage you did. But you can stand it. Any other year we could have stood it, too. But this year—" She stopped, wishing she could call back the words. Her father wouldn't like her asking for pity, even from Ted.

Ted touched Sade's shoulder with a gentle hand. "Easy, old girl," he said soothingly. "Can't she find her way around at all without him?"

Cindy sighed. "She could if she'd try. But she won't even stand still and let me look after her. Honest, Ted, she just acts crazy. At first she was pretty good. She kept calling him, and she seemed always waiting for him to come back. I thought she'd give that up pretty soon, and then she'd start learning how to get around by herself. She did give up waiting, but now she's bound to run off looking for Tom. No matter how I watch her, or what I do, she manages to break loose. She doesn't even try to take things easy or feel her way. Just tears off and bangs into anything that's in her way. Never seems to care if she hurts herself or not. She'll kill herself if she doesn't stop it."

Ted said comfortingly, "You're doing your best, Cindy. It won't do her any good for you to get yourself all upset about it."

Cindy blinked hard to hold back tears, but she couldn't quite keep the quaver out of her voice. "You know how I always felt about my white team. But Tom was my favorite. When I thought Dad might sell them, it was Tom I worried about missing. Now that I have to watch Sade breaking her heart over him—oh, it's so sad, Ted. Isn't it?"

"Well—sure it is. But you can't worry your life away over a horse. It doesn't make sense."

"I know," Cindy admitted. "Maybe because there was nobody I could talk to about it, and I couldn't get it out of my mind. If my mother were here, we would have talked about it. Maybe she could have thought of something to do. But then, if she were here it wouldn't have happened at all."

"You don't know that," Ted reminded her. "Anyway, she can't help being sick. How about your father? Can't you talk to him?"

Cindy shook her head. "If I told him how I worry about Sade he'd think I was blaming him for selling Tom. And I know he couldn't help it. Anyway, since that time we thought Mama was coming home, he doesn't talk even as much as he used to. Just glooms around, and if I say anything to him he doesn't even answer. Only when we get a letter from her he cheers up for a little while. But that never lasts long. Because she writes these long letters, all about how much she loves us and everything. But she never says anything about when she's going to come home. And she could, Ted! She could, if she only wanted to."

Ted looked shocked. "You shouldn't say a thing like that, Cindy. You know it isn't so, don't you?"

"Yes, I guess I do. But that's what Dad thinks. He

doesn't say so, but I know that's what he's thinking. And he doesn't blame her. He blames himself."

Ted shook his head. "No wonder you get to feeling low. But everything's going to work out all right. You wait and see if it doesn't. Your mother's just waiting until her doctor tells her she can come home. Pretty soon she'll be back here, and she'll get everybody cheered up in a hurry. Right now, you'd better just think about taking care of your old mare. And if you get down in the dumps again, come over and tell me your troubles. All right?"

"All right." Cindy smiled gratefully.

She went on doing her best for Sade. She brought her apples and lumps of sugar, patted her, talked to her. Over and over she told Sade, "You can remember where things are if you try. You can get along without him. You should be glad he's gone. The silly, conceited, lazy old rascal! Always trying to fool you into doing his share of the work. And then stealing from you, too. You remember that, don't you? Anyway, he's forgotten all about you now, so you might as well forget about him."

But of course Sade couldn't understand, and Cindy had a feeling that even if she could have understood every word she wouldn't have believed it. In spite of all Cindy's care, she became every day more wild and reckless in her distracted seeking. Every day she seemed to neigh more loudly and more frantically, and to listen with more breathless intensity for an answer.

Cindy's heart ached with pity, for she knew there could never be an answer. Tom would never come back.

Some nights, after she had tied Sade in her stall, Cindy would sit at the supper table dazed with weariness. Her eyes would be so blurred with sleep that her father's face would fade and change and lose its shape, until it seemed that it was Sade's long, mournful white countenance that confronted her across the table. Then, as she blinked, and sharply shook her head to bring her father back into focus, she would find herself thinking that there was something in his face very much like Sade's mixture of sadness, bewilderment, and anger.

Like Sade, he was what was left of a broken team. Like her, he was angry at the world for taking away the one he loved and needed. Angry at the world, because he didn't know who to blame. Because no person was to blame. It was just the way things happened.

16 : Planning a Surprise

Time passed, and it was November. The days were shorter. Mostly the skies were gray. Chilly winds blew, and now and then brought with them bursts of thin, icy rain.

Dad kept a fire going all the time in the range, so that the kitchen was warm although the rest of the house wasn't. They sat there in the evenings after supper, reading by the light of the lamp that burned dim and smoky no matter how often Dad trimmed the wick. Cindy had read all the books in the house except a few that looked hopelessly dull, and all the books in the small library at school. Now she was reading some of the best ones over again.

Her father read mostly farm magazines, and booklets about farming he had written to Washington for. Cindy remembered the way he used to read them—quickly, with gleaming eyes, once in a while calling to her mother to listen to something about a new variety of clover or a better design for a hog feeder. He used to borrow her mother's sewing scissors and clip out pieces about such things, putting them away in a box on the little table in the corner. She could see the box now, still sitting in its place close to where the telephone used to be before they had it taken out. The clippings protruding raggedly from the top of the box were covered thickly with dust. Dad never read anything aloud now, or clipped anything out. He spent most of the time just looking at the page with dull, empty eyes.

Often in the evening Cindy would fall asleep, and her head would drop down onto her open book. Then her father would shake her awake and tell her to go to bed. She would stumble sleepily up the stairs and fall quickly asleep again.

On the second Saturday in November, Cindy was holding Sade for her father while he tended a cut on her chest. She had made it the day before when she flung herself against the barbed wire near the watering trough. Now thick, dark blood was oozing through the white hair, and the skin around it showed through, pink and puffy.

Dad held his knife for a moment in the flame of a match, then used it to make a small cut in the skin. His hands were gentle, his face soft with pity. Sade winced at the first touch of the knife.

"Whoa, girl, whoa!" Dad said coaxingly. "Sure, I know it hurts. Poor old Sade. Easy, now. That's right."

Strange, Cindy thought, that her father could speak so gently and understandingly to animals. Yet with people he so often wouldn't, or couldn't, say what was in his mind.

When Dad took some warm water in a small syringe and washed it into the opening he had made, Cindy held tighter to Sade's halter rope, expecting her to struggle against the painful treatment. But Sade just stood droopily, her lower lip hanging. Lately her ribs had begun to show through along her sides, and the hollows above her eyes had deepened sharply. She looked very old.

"She looks awful." Cindy didn't want to say it, but suddenly she couldn't hold back the words. "Do you think she'll die?"

Her father shook his head impatiently. "She's not hurt much."

"But she's getting so thin. She hardly eats at all. She seems to be mad all the time—angry, I mean."

Dad dropped the syringe into a pan of water. He looked at Sade and nodded. "Yes, I guess she does. She hates the whole world since Tom's gone. Because she doesn't know who to blame for taking him away. If she were smart, she'd kick my head off."

"But you couldn't help it," Cindy protested. "You had to."

"There was a time I wouldn't have done it," her father said slowly. "Not for anything."

"It was Ben Thompson's fault," Cindy said bitterly. "I hate him."

"Cindy!" Her father looked down at her, and for the first time in a long while he seemed really to see her. "No, you mustn't do that. It's not good for you to hate people. Try to understand that Ben Thompson is a little like Sade, himself. Alone, and mad at the world. Why, he's worse off than any of us. You know what day this is?"

Cindy thought for a moment. "November the thirteenth. Why?"

"It's Ben Thompson's birthday. Years ago an old fellow who was put out about something Ben had done said to me, 'Well, what can you expect from somebody who was born on Friday the thirteenth? And in November, too, the most miserable month of the year?' That struck me so funny I've remembered it ever since. Expect Ben must be seventy or more today. Wonder how long it's been since anybody wished him a happy birthday."

Later, as she and her father went silently about their usual Saturday washing and cleaning, Cindy kept thinking about Ben Thompson. It was strange to think of that dour old man having a birthday. But of course everybody had to have one. It was hard to imagine that once he had been a baby, jolly and cute like all babies. Then a little boy, like Davy. Then a bigger boy, like Ted. Then a young man, getting married. Something had happened to change him from the nice little baby to the man whose wife couldn't put up with his stinginess. Then, in the long years of being alone, he must have grown worse and worse.

Cindy shuddered to think how awful it must have been, spending so many years alone. So many years when there was nobody even to remember when his birthday came. She had hated Ben Thompson for a long time, but now she began to feel sorry for him. Then she had an idea.

The more she thought about the idea, the better it seemed. She remembered a story she had read, about a little girl and a cross old woman she hated. For some reason the little girl had started to feel sorry for the

old woman, and had taken her a Christmas present.
The cross old woman had been so delighted that she had
left the little girl all her property when she died.

Cindy's heart began to beat faster with excitement.
A birthday should be even better than Christmas, because it was a privately special day for every person.
She would bake Ben Thompson a birthday cake. Surely
not even he could help feeling kindly toward her after
that. Surely he would want to do her some favor in
return. And what she wanted from him was such a little
thing. Not to be left all his property, or even part of
it. Just to have Tom back.

For nearly a year one bad thing after another had
happened, and there had never been anything Cindy
could do to stop them. Now here was something she
could do, and such an easy thing. But she wouldn't
tell her father. It would be a secret, and a surprise.
When he got out the truck for the weekly trip to town
she said, "Is it all right if I don't go along today? I'm
sort of tired."

"Of course you don't have to go if you don't feel like
it." He gave her a searching look, then put a hand
lightly on her forehead. "You're not sick? Maybe I
should have the doctor take a look at you."

"No, I feel fine. Honest I do." She couldn't blame her
father for suspecting something wrong. It was the first
time she had ever turned down a chance to go anywhere
with him.

When he was gone, Cindy hurried into the house. She
put more wood on the fire, and adjusted the draft so
that the oven would get good and hot. Then she looked

through her mother's recipe file for her favorite cake. It was easy to tell which had been most used, for the card on which it was written was worn and dog-eared, disfigured with fingerprints and marred with a blurry patch where some liquid had splashed onto it.

Cindy frowned over the list of ingredients, written in her mother's big, sprawling hand. Flour. Sugar. Butter. Milk. She measured them one after the other into the biggest bowl she could find. The sugar was the last in the house. The butter, fresh out of the chilly cellar, was very hard.

But then came a problem. Whatever had splashed on the card had made the last half of the next lines impossible to read. What could "3 tsp. bak—" be? She peered into the cabinet for something that began with "bak." Of course! Baking soda. She dug out three generously heaped spoons full and dumped them into the bowl.

Then, "1 tsp. v—" What began with a v? At once she answered herself. Vinegar. It was a little hard to get a teaspoonful out of a gallon jug, but she managed without too much spilling.

The last line said plainly, "6 egg whites." Cindy had often watched her mother separating egg whites from their yolks, and it looked easy. She found it wasn't. The first yolk pierced itself against a jagged edge of shell and joined the white in the bowl. The same thing happened on the second try, except that several pieces of shell went along. After that she was reasonably successful, and when she had fished out all the pieces of shell she could find, she hoped that the two yolks wouldn't make much difference among so many other things.

Mixing wasn't as easy as it looked when her mother did it, either. Cindy stirred until her arms ached, and the result still didn't look like the smooth, creamy batter she had seen her mother pour into the pans. It was darker, and full of lumps. But it would have to do. She scraped it into the two round pans and slid it into the oven.

It was astonishing that the making of one cake should have left so many dirty bowls, cups, and spoons. Besides that, the table and even the floor around it was powdered with flour, smeared with butter, and spattered with little dribbles of egg.

Absorbed in cleaning up, Cindy forgot about looking at the cake until a strong smell of scorching reminded her. Then she burned her hand on the side of the oven while taking it out. But at least it was done. She tried not to wonder about its strange appearance, oddly flat except for several walnut-sized bumps. She told herself that it would even out as it cooled.

But it didn't even out. Even after Cindy had taken the layers out of the pans, replaced the chunks that had stuck and had to be pried off with a knife, and pared off a few parts that were badly scorched, it looked as bumpy as ever.

Seafoam icing seemed to be the only kind that could be made without white sugar. Cindy was surprisingly successful with a large batch. But when she had plastered this liberally between the layers and all over the surface, filling in the cracks and leveling off the bumpy top, she was reassured. It was quite a good-looking cake, after all.

She pulled a chair up to the tall cupboard beside the stove, and searched the top shelf. In the box of candles her mother had bought for Marcy's last birthday cake, there were four left. Not nearly enough, but they would serve as tokens that this was a birthday cake. She stuck them into the icing, in the form of a square. On the cardboard back of one of her used school tablets she printed in black crayon, *Happy Birthday, Mr. Thompson,* and propped it against the side of the cake. Then she stood back and nodded with satisfaction. Later she would take it over to Ben Thompson's house.

She imagined his surprise when he opened the door and saw her there, with the birthday cake in her hands. She would say, "Mr. Thompson, I just happened to find out that this is your birthday. Happy birthday, Mr. Thompson!" She shivered with excitement, just thinking about it.

17 : Tom Gets His Way

Cindy was so absorbed in imagining the happy surprise that would come over old Ben's face when he saw his birthday cake, that she didn't hear the noise of the truck in the driveway, or the sound of heavy footsteps on the walk. The first thing she heard was Ben Thompson's voice, shrill and rasping with anger, just outside.

She ran to the door, opened it a crack and peered out. After her fantasy of a happy, smiling Ben, the sight of the real Ben was like the shock of hitting hard ground when the rope you've been swinging on suddenly breaks. She wanted to run and hide. Instead, she stepped through the door and closed it behind her. Trembling, she watched and listened. Neither Ben nor her father seemed to know that she was there.

The two men stood on the little back porch, glaring at each other. Ben Thompson's face was red, his pale eyes bulged, his whole skinny body shook. Cindy's father looked a little angry too, but more puzzled and surprised. Cindy's breath choked in her throat. What terrible thing had happened now?

Ben Thompson shook a gnarled finger under her father's nose. "Thought you told me that was a gentle horse!" he shrieked.

"I did. And he is."

Ben gave a violent snort and stamped one foot so hard that the floor boards cracked under the shock. "Horse is a devil!" he shouted. "I wasn't surprised when he tried to run home every chance he got. Happens, now and again, with new stock. But you know what else he did? Kicked down the side of his stall. Tramped down my fence and got in my one good patch of soybeans. Tore and stomped around and ruined the whole works. You know that other white gelding, the mate I had for him? He's scared the living daylights out of that poor critter. Takes out after him every time he sees him, ready to tear him apart. And now what does he do? Tries to kill me, that's what! Had him tied in the barn. Went in to feed him, and he was loose. He's a devil, I tell you. Kicked at me. Barely missed me. Knocked the hat right off my head. Then took after me with his teeth. Ready to tear me to pieces, you could see it in his eyes. I just barely got away. Slammed the door to, left him in there ripping the place apart."

Cindy listened with disbelief, and then with a terrible joy. Those were the same tricks Tom had played here, pretending to be fierce and mean when really he was the gentlest horse alive. Here he couldn't fool even the calves. But he had surely scared old Ben, and she was proud of him.

Still, it didn't really seem like Tom. Here, he had been good as gold most of the time, just once in a while breaking loose with one of his pranks. At Ben Thompson's place, he had been on his worst behavior and never good at all. Almost as if— But, of course. Tom hadn't cared that Ben's place was better and more comfortable than the Martins', or been glad to escape from the never-ending task of watching over Sade. He hadn't come close to forgetting her. He had been trying constantly, in the only way he knew, to get back to her.

Cindy's father said, "I don't know, Ben. That doesn't sound like Tom. I'll admit he used to get me mad plenty of times with his tricks, but I never knew him to do a really mean thing. I'll tell you what. I'll go over with you and see if I can calm him down."

"Calm him down, nothing!" Ben growled. "I got my gun out to shoot him, that's what I did."

Cindy just managed to choke off a scream of horror.

"Changed my mind, though," Ben went on. "Got a lot of money tied up in that horse. Dave, you committed a bare-faced fraud when you sold him. I ought to take you to court. Sue you for misrepresentation. Why, I don't know but what it's a prison offense to sell a man a dangerous animal like that. But I'll let you off easy. You give me my money and you take back your horse."

"I'd be glad to, Ben," Dave Martin said slowly. "But I don't know where I'd get that much money right now. I paid what you gave me on a couple of notes I owed at the bank. You'll have to give me a little time."

"Time? That murdering horse you sold me didn't give me any time. You get me that money next week, or I'll have you in court for it. And right now, you go get that plagued animal out of my barn."

"All right. Let's go." Cindy's father turned and started down the steps.

Ben Thompson shook his head. "No, sir! I'll wait

right here until I see him back in your pasture. I'm not going near my place while that devil's there."

"Whatever you say, Ben."

Cindy watched her father disappear down the lane, to walk across the fields in the direction of Thompson's place. She felt shaky with relief, and wild with happiness. Soon now, Tom would be back with Sade, where he belonged. It was almost too good to believe.

Ben Thompson was still standing on the porch, looking out at the chilly grayness of the afternoon where the thin, cold rain was beginning to fall again. At last Cindy remembered her manners.

"Won't you come and sit inside, Mr. Thompson?" she invited. "It will take Dad a while, and you might as well be warm."

"Guess I might as well."

When they got inside, there was the birthday cake on the kitchen table. Cindy stopped short in dismay. She had forgotten all about that cake. She couldn't imagine now why she had done such a silly thing as to make it. All her kindly thoughts of Ben had vanished when she heard the terrible things he had said about Tom. And when he had accused her father of cheating him, she had hated him more than ever.

She marched to the stove and took as long as she could putting unnecessary wood onto the fire. Then she went to the sink and washed her hands. Finally, unable to think of anything else to do, she sat down in a chair as far away from Ben as she could. Still, Ben hadn't said a word. It was too much to hope that he hadn't noticed the cake. At last she stole a look at him.

He was still standing halfway between the door and the table, looking straight at the cake. On his face was an expression of bewilderment and suspicion. He looked at Cindy and pointed a finger at the cake. "You make that?" he demanded.

Cindy nodded, speechless with embarrassment.

"Why?"

Cindy cleared her throat and said shakily, "I— Dad mentioned it was your birthday. And I thought—you didn't have anybody to make you one."

"Hm. Well— You going to cut me a piece? Take one for yourself, too."

"You've got to light the candles first," Cindy reminded him.

"All right. Fetch me a match and I will."

The warm glow of the flames gave Ben's old face a soft, rosy look. The tiny fires reflected in his eyes made them twinkle warmly. In spite of herself, Cindy's friendly feelings for the old man began to return. No matter why he had done it, he had given Tom back. And he was pleased with his birthday cake. Though he hadn't said so, she could tell he was.

"Now make a wish, and then blow out the candles," she reminded him.

He snorted. "Me make a wish? I'm too old for that nonsense." He sucked in a deep breath, puffed hard, and out went all four candles.

Cindy got out plates and forks, and cut each of them a big piece of cake. She poured each of them a glass of milk. Too excited to be hungry, she watched Ben

Thompson cut off a chunk of cake and pop it into his mouth.

"Ahrg! Ugh!" Ben let out a half-choked roar, leaped from his chair, and dashed out the door. A moment later he reappeared. He stood in the doorway, pointing at Cindy with a trembling finger. "Trying to poison me!" he shrilled. "I'll have you and your father both in court, you see if I don't." And he disappeared, slamming the door behind him.

Cindy was stunned with horror. Everything had been going so well. Old Ben had seemed pleased. Then— what in the world had happened? Had she really put poison in the cake without knowing it? She imagined herself in a courtroom, accused of trying to poison Ben Thompson. Everyone was looking at her as they might at some dreadful, venomous snake. There was no way she could convince them she hadn't meant to do it.

Through her despair she heard a knocking at the door. Cindy stared wide-eyed, unable to speak. The door opened slowly. Mrs. Nichols came in. Her plump face was flushed, and she was dabbing at her eyes with a handkerchief.

She dropped into a chair across from where Cindy sat, and slowly shook her head. "Cindy!" she said accusingly. "What in the world did you put in that cake?"

In a voice breathless with haste and flat with hopelessness, Cindy told Mrs. Nichols everything—exactly how she had made the cake, everything that had happened until the moment when Ben Thompson slammed the door angrily behind him.

"And then he said he was going to take me to court for poisoning him," Cindy concluded despairingly.

Mrs. Nichols leaned across the table and took Cindy's hand in a warm, firm grip. "Don't you worry about that. I laughed him out of that poisoning notion—if he ever really had it. But he still thinks you cooked up something special to get even with him about Tom. Says if it was an accident you surely need some cooking lessons."

Mrs. Nichols broke off a piece of cake and nibbled it cautiously. She frowned, took a bigger bite, and made a pained face. "Can't say I blame him," she said. But the twinkle in her blue eyes took most of the sting out of the words.

"The first thing you did wrong, Cindy, was to use baking soda instead of baking powder. They're both good for making things rise. But baking soda only works when you use certain other things with it—sour milk, or brown sugar, or chocolate. Your second mistake was not sifting the dry things together. Your soda was lumpy, and it didn't get mixed in well with the flour and sugar. Ben Thompson bit into a lump of soda, and if you'd ever done that you'd understand how he could think he'd been poisoned. The third thing you did wrong was to put in that vinegar where it should have been vanilla. Wherever that got to the soda, it made the soda start to work. But that was only in spots, and that's why you had lumps on the top."

Cindy sighed. "I don't know how I could be so stupid."

Mrs. Nichols laughed. "Now, don't feel bad. I fed

worse to Mr. Nichols when we were first married. You know, and I think I told you this before, I never learned to cook or keep house when I was a girl, any more than you. It seemed stupid and tiresome to me. I never thought I'd get married, when I was your age. I used to ride pretty well, and I used to dream about joining up with a Wild West show. Annie Oakley was my idol."

Cindy leaned eagerly across the table. "That's what I used to think. That women's work was stupid and tire-some, and not important anyway. I never wanted to learn anything about it. But since Mama's been gone, nothing goes right. Nothing's comfortable the way it used to be. Dad's not the same as he used to be. I'm not. Nothing's the same without her. It makes me wish I'd learned how to do some of the things she used to do for us."

"I think that's a good idea." Mrs. Nichols beamed. "But, my heavens! I've been sitting here talking to you longer than I meant to. I just stopped in to ask you and your father to come over and have supper with us. Mr. Nichols is waiting outside in the car. You get your coat and come along. Your father should be here any minute. He's had plenty of time to get to Ben's place and back."

Cindy hurried into her coat and followed Mrs. Nichols toward the Nichols' car, parked near the barn. Far away down the road, she could see the little patch of white that was Tom, with her father on his back. She ran into the barn, untied Sade's halter rope with fumbling haste, and led her outside.

She could see that Tom was moving at a quick trot,

his head held high. Then she heard his clear, loud neigh. Sade's ears strained forward. Her whole body began to tremble. She answered, her call lower-pitched, imploring. Cindy braced herself and held the halter rope tight. But Sade didn't move. After a moment the trembling stopped. She stood quietly, her head raised, with a calm, expectant look.

Cindy's father reined Tom in, slipped down off his back and removed his bridle. Then he stood back while Tom trotted over to Sade, stretched out his pearl-gray nose to touch hers gently, then turned and stood beside her in the old way. Then, just as he had always done, Tom turned and walked slowly toward the watering trough. Sade moved with him. Side by side, they stood to drink. Then, when Cindy had opened the gate, they went through it and down the lane. Just as always, Sade's nose rested lightly on Tom's flank. Just as always, her step was steady and confident.

18 : A Team Pulls Together

Mr. Nichols had gotten out of the car, and all four of them stood together, watching Tom and Sade until they were out of sight. Cindy looked up at her father. His face had a softened, happy look.

Mrs. Nichols said, "My! Doesn't it do your heart good to see them back together?"

Mr. Nichols nodded. "Too bad Ben Thompson didn't stay around and watch. Might have made him realize what a mean thing it was to try to split up a team that depended on each other as much as those two. Just because he heard there was a firm in the city willing to pay a fancy price for a well-matched white team to pull a delivery wagon."

"So that was why he wanted Tom!" Cindy's father exclaimed. "I thought it was pure spite and meanness. Just to show me there was no combination in the world that couldn't be split up."

Mr. Nichols chuckled. "Why, no, Dave. Ben wouldn't go out of his way to spite you. He likes you, as much as he likes anybody. He admires your independence, and the way you run your place. I've heard him say you'd make more money than any farmer in the county before you were through, because you had the patience to lay a good foundation and the brains to do things right. He did think you were soft for hanging onto that blind mare, but so did a lot of other people. He never learned there's got to be some softness in this world. I hate to think what life would be like if there wasn't."

"If Ben had taken Sade too," Cindy's father said, "chances are Tom would have behaved fine. I've never had any trouble getting him to work with another horse. The difference was, he knew Sade would be there waiting for him when he got through. I thought I knew horses, but this has surely surprised me. I could figure where Sade, the weak one, would be no good by herself. What I never expected was that the strong one would turn out to be worthless, too, as soon as he was alone. Common sense would tell you he could do twice as much when he wasn't tied down to a helpless creature like her."

Mrs. Nichols looked thoughtful. "I don't think it's the first time Ben's hardheadedness has cost him something. A long time ago, it cost him a good wife. Don't expect him to admit he's been wrong this time, any more than he ever admitted he was wrong then. But he knows.

" 'Judge not,' the Bible tells us. So we've got to take Ben the way he is, not the way we'd like him to be. He's hard-working and honest, and stingy as he is he's never refused to do his part when somebody really needed a hand. Remember when the Cuthberts were burned out a couple of years ago? Ben put in two hundred dollars and a good cow, toward putting them on their feet again."

"That's right," Mr. Nichols admitted. "And then

he took all the good out of it by growling about how the county would be better off without a bunch that was too shiftless to put lightning rods on their barn. But I guess we've got more to do than stand here gossiping about the neighbors. Dave, I hope you won't mind if my wife takes Cindy along with her for a bit. I'll give you a hand with your chores. Something I want to talk over with you."

Mrs. Nichols drove slowly and with great caution, so that it took them longer than Cindy would have believed possible to cover the half mile between their two houses. But, even considering that, they met a surprising lot of traffic on the road—two wagons, two trucks, and a passenger car. If things kept up this way it would soon be as bad as the city, Cindy thought.

She followed Mrs. Nichols up the walk, through the big screened porch, into the kitchen with its warmth and its sweet and spicy smells. It was nearly dark inside, except for a flicker of ruddy light from the narrow openings in the front of the stove.

Mrs. Nichols called softly, "Ted?"

"I'm right here." The voice came from the next room, and was quickly followed by the dim shape of Ted in the doorway.

"Surprise, Cindy!" Mrs. Nichols announced. "Ted made me promise he'd be here when I showed you." There was a click, and the room was full of light.

Cindy caught her breath with amazement. Electric lights! Here, on a farm outside Walnut Grove. Light in an instant, without striking a match, without trimming a wick, without any smell of kerosene. Light that reached into every corner, better than the sunshine of the brightest day.

"Isn't this great, Cindy?" Ted's blue eyes were sparkling with pleasure. "And just wait till you see what else! Mom's got an electric machine to wash clothes in. And that's just the beginning. Now that we have the electricity, there will be lots of other things we can use with it. Next she's getting an electric iron. Just one iron, and all you do is plug it into the socket and it stays hot as long as you need it. Pretty soon we'll have a refrigerator, a toaster, lights in the barn, maybe even a milking machine. Boy!" He grinned ecstatically.

"Just like living in town," Cindy managed to say in an awe-stricken voice. "How in the world did you get it? Dad said it costs a fortune, putting up the line to get electricity way out here."

"We make our own," Ted explained. "It's one of those home generators that runs on gasoline. And don't think we didn't wait a long time to get it. Mom's been saving her egg money for years, and then we all put in anything we make extra. I put in half of my trapping money, so it's part mine. Isn't it, Mom?"

"That's right. We all did it together. Now we can all enjoy it together."

"That's wonderful." Cindy voice didn't sound as enthusiastic as she would have liked it to. Though she was ashamed of the feeling, she couldn't overcome the bitter jealousy and resentment she felt. Couldn't Ted and his mother understand how cruel it was to make her feel more keenly than ever the contrast between the fortunate and happy Nichols family and the lonely and defeated Martins?

"Don't you see, Cindy?" Ted chattered on excitedly. "People don't have to live the way they did fifty years ago, just because their homes are in the country. We can have things just as nice as in town—nicer, because there's room here for trees and animals, and good places to play and go swimming."

"Yes, that's right." Cindy wished her grandparents could be here, to see the Nichols' farmhouse looking as bright and cheerful as their city home. Maybe they'd admit they'd been wrong when they thought the only way anybody could have a comfortable life was to move to town.

"Ted, would you make sure the windows in the chicken house are closed? I think it's going to turn cold tonight," Mrs. Nichols said.

"Sure, Mom." Ted went out quickly.

"I'll help." Cindy started to get to her feet, but Mrs. Nichols shook her head.

"No, Cindy. You stay here. I want to talk to you. There's an idea I've been turning over in my mind, and I want to see what you think of it. I asked Ted, and he liked it fine. But whether we do anything about it is up to you."

Cindy was pleased at the idea of Ted and his mother thinking of something they could do with her, or for her. Then she remembered her father, and how he felt about taking favors you couldn't repay. Whatever this plan was, chances were she'd have to refuse it. But at least she could listen, and be grateful for what they had wanted to do.

"Soon your mother will be coming home," Mrs. Nichols said. "Have you thought about what's going to happen then?"

"Things will be just the way they used to be, of course," Cindy answered.

Mrs. Nichols shook her head. "Things are never just the way they used to be. They won't be this time, for sure. Do you expect your mother to be able to cook and wash and clean and sew the way she always did? Is that what you want her for?"

"Of course not!" Cindy was indignant. "Dad and I know she probably can't do any work at all for a while, and never as much as she used to. Just to have her be there is all we want. Dad and I will do all the work, just the way we've done while she's been away."

"But there will be much more work, with your mother there, and Marcella and little David too. You'll never be able to find the time. And besides, you don't know how. Would you want your mother to live the way you and your father have lived this past year?"

Cindy thought of the cold, comfortless house and the hurried, unappetizing meals. Her eyes filled with tears, but she said with desperate determination, "We'll manage somehow."

"Oh, Cindy!" Mrs. Nichols cried remorsefully. "I didn't mean to discourage you. I'm just leading up to my plan, and here it is.

"If you could take most of the housework off your mother's shoulders she could come home sooner, couldn't she? And be surer of staying well when she does come?"

"Yes."

Mrs. Nichols went on. "While she's been gone you've been working outside with your father, and doing a fine job. I don't know how he'd have managed without you. But you must know most of that work is too rough and heavy for you. No matter how hard you try, you just aren't strong enough to do as much as you'd like to. Isn't that right?"

Cindy nodded, blinking back tears of anger and frustration.

"Well," Mrs. Nichols said triumphantly, "here's Ted big and strong enough to do all those things that are so hard for you. He's just wasting his time around here, because his father and the older boys have all the jobs laid out for themselves. Ted runs my errands and does my chores because I haven't got a girl to help me, but he'd rather be doing man's work. Now, why don't you and Ted trade jobs? You come over and help me, after school and Saturdays until your mother comes home, and I'll teach you how to run a house. Ted will help your father in his time off, and your father will teach him how to run a farm. We'll all be pulling together, with each of us doing the things he can do best. That's the way to get things done. What do you say?"

Cindy had had polite words of refusal ready for the gift or favor she was expecting Mrs. Nichols to offer. But she couldn't speak them now. Suspiciously, she turned the plan over and over in her mind, but there seemed to be no reason for objecting to it. It was a trade, and one that had good in it for everybody. She said cautiously, "If it's all right with Dad, I'd like to."

Mrs. Nichols set her lips grimly. "Your father is going to listen to reason for once, or the whole county will want to know the reason why. He should be here any minute for supper, so you can ask him. Now, Cindy, you help me set the table and finish things off."

Mrs. Nichols was showing Cindy how to thicken gravy without making lumps in it, when they heard the truck coming noisily up the drive. A moment later Mr. Nichols came into the kitchen, followed by Cindy's father, and then by Ted.

Ted and his father were smiling. Cindy's father had a strangely subdued and doubtful look. He stood for a moment just inside the door, looking at Cindy. Then he too began to smile.

Mrs. Nichols rushed across the floor and took one of his hands in both of hers. She said in a voice shaky with emotion, "Everything's all right, isn't it, Dave? If we hadn't all been so pigheaded we could have worked this out a long time ago."

With a smile she turned to her husband. "Fred, you must have done some fast talking to convince him. I half expected him to throw you off his place."

Mr. Nichols grinned. "We ganged up on him. Managed to get things timed so neighbors were swarming in from all directions at once. Everybody was primed with the same idea—your idea in the first place, but one they all wondered why they'd never thought of themselves. If you can pitch in to help a man who's been burned out or flooded out, why can't you pitch in to help a man who's lost half his family for a year? Put it that way, and if Dave was to refuse it would be the same as saying that a wife and two young ones weren't worth much. So everything's set. Material all on hand, labor all pledged. The job ought to be done within a week."

"Wh—what job?" Cindy faltered.

"You mean you haven't told her yet?" Mr. Nichols looked at his wife reproachfully. "Why, Cindy, the job of putting electric lights and hot and cold running water and a new furnace in your house, that's what. Making the place all nice and snug and fit for your mother to live in, so she can come home and let your father put his mind back to farming again.

"Harry Summers down south of town donated the generator he's had sitting around since he put in a bigger one a couple of months ago. That was the biggest item. We got the bathroom fixtures they took out of the old Raymond house when they tore it down. A pretty good furnace Al Russell says we can have if we get it out of his cellar. It's been doing nothing for a couple of years, ever since he put in the gas heat. Plus a lot of other odds and ends, and a few dollars folks chipped in for things we might have to buy. Got forty-three people putting in a day or two of work, including an electrician and a plumber. Why, even the preacher gave a day. After he opens the proceedings with a prayer, he's going to help dig the ditches for the water pipes. And—say, I almost forgot! Old Ben Thompson got curious when he saw the crowd and came back to see what was going on. When he found out, he said he'd do his part by calling that horse of yours a free gift. Said after nearly getting himself killed trying to keep a couple of horses apart, he wasn't going to have anybody think he'd try to keep a human family from getting together. So there you are! And if the arrangement with the young people works out all right—"

"What arrangement is that?" Cindy's father demanded.

Eagerly Cindy explained. When she had finished her father said, "That makes good sense. If it suits you and Ted it suits me just fine."

"Pst! Cindy!" Ted moved close to her, and while the older people talked on about furnaces and electric wiring, they carried on their own low-voiced conversation. "Pretty good, huh? Getting me a real job? You think I can do things to suit your father?"

"Of course!" Cindy said. "It's going to help him a lot, having somebody as strong as you around. He won't need to stop what he's doing and lift something that's too heavy or reach something that's too high, the way he did all the time for me. I know he'll want to start paying you as soon as he can. Guess it won't be much fun to work for nothing."

"Sure it will!" Ted grinned broadly. "I'll be learning, won't I? And anyway, I wouldn't get paid if I worked around here, so what's the difference?"

"Well, if it suits you—" Cindy looked quickly up at Ted, and then down at the table again. She had been thinking how nice it would be to have Ted at their place every day working with her father. It seemed to her that he must be able to read the thought in her eyes, and that inside himself he would be laughing at her silliness.

Ted said in a husky, uncertain voice, "Cindy—"

She glanced at him quickly again. His face was very red. "What's the matter, Ted?"

"Uh— Nothing. I was just thinking. You know— Well, we're having our first basketball game next Friday, against Millport. I'll be playing on the freshman team, in the warm-up game. So Mom says if you'd like to, you're welcome to ride over with us and go to the game. Would you?"

Cindy's heart beat faster and faster as she listened. Her throat was so dry, that it was hard to speak. "Well —I don't know. It's nice of your mother to offer. But— maybe if I went along with your family, and your friends noticed, they might think—"

"Think you were my girl?" Ted laughed. "Oh, I guess I could stand it. A fellow doesn't mind too much being teased about a girl, if she's pretty."

Just then Cindy's father decided it was time for them to go home. She was glad of that, because she could leave without saying another word. She just smiled at Ted, so that he would know her answer was yes. And all the way home those last words sang themselves over and over again in her head. "If she's pretty, if she's pretty."

When Cindy and her father were home, she ran straight from the door to get pen and ink and paper. She laid them on the kitchen table and turned to her father. "Please," she said huskily, "write to her now."

Her father sat down at the table. He picked up the

pen, dipped it into the ink, wrote, *Dear Lucy,* and laid it down again. He looked at Cindy helplessly. "Suppose I tell her about all this, and she still doesn't come home?"

"Oh, you don't want to tell her!" Cindy cried. "It's got to be a surprise. It would spoil everything if you told her. Just ask her to come."

"But I have asked her," her father said, with a puzzled frown. "I've asked her a dozen times."

"I'll bet you never have," Cindy said boldly. "You've asked her when she'd come, and you've told her she ought to. But you've never really asked her to."

He frowned, with a look of thinking hard. "Maybe not, in so many words. What difference does that make?"

"I'll bet it would make plenty of difference," Cindy said. "What do you think made Tom so anxious to get back here that he almost scared Ben Thompson into shooting him?"

"Why—because of Sade, of course. He knew she couldn't get along without him. Although if anybody had told me a horse could know a thing like that, much less do anything about it, I'd have said he was crazy."

"So if it works that way for a horse, don't you think it would work even more for a person?" Cindy demanded. "I believe the best thing in the world is to know somebody needs you. It makes you feel strong and important, so you can do things you never thought you could do."

"Yes," her father said, "it surely does."

"We've never let Mama feel important," Cindy went

on earnestly. "We've kept on telling her how well we were getting along, managing everything without her, and perfectly happy."

Slowly, Cindy's father shook his head. "I didn't want to worry her. I didn't want to coax her to come back before she was able."

"I know. And it was right at first, when she was awfully sick. But now— Maybe she's afraid to come home. Maybe she thinks she'd only make things harder for us if she isn't strong enough to do all she used to do."

"I couldn't let her go on thinking that." Dave Martin looked down at his big, calloused hands, then up at Cindy. "It's not easy to say what you feel, when all your life you've been used to holding it in. But now I've got to. I never thought about her needing to be told. I guess I always just expected her to know." With a look of determination he picked up the pen, dipped it into the ink and began to write.

Cindy watched the frown on her father's face soften and disappear as he wrote. She heard the pen scratch slowly at first, then faster and faster. She knew now, as surely as she knew that the sun would come up tomorrow morning, that before many days had passed her mother would be back.

Marcy and Davy would be back, too, she remembered. She wondered whether they would be happy here. They had changed so much during the months in town. They were soft and smug and spoiled and selfish, both of them, she thought resentfully. But maybe she would have been just the same, she realized suddenly, if she had lived so long in a place where everything was done for her and nobody needed her help.

When they were home before, Marcy had had her work to do. She had put the silverware on the table, dried it and put it away, helped with the dusting and cleaning. Even Davy, though hardly more than a baby, had helped feed the chickens and bring in the wood. When they came home again they must have those things to do, and more because they were bigger now. They'd be able to feel like part of a team again, important to pull their share of the load.

So, Cindy thought with surprise, this idea of a team was bigger than just two horses or two people. It could be a whole family. Or a whole neighborhood, working together to help someone. It could be a whole country. Maybe some day it could even be the whole world.

Cindy stopped short at the magnitude of this idea, and went back to picturing the way things were going to be for herself and her family. As she sat there with her head bowed in thought, the soft waves of her wheat-colored hair fell forward and brushed cheeks pink with a flush of happiness. Her solemn gray eyes and the firmness of her mouth and chin seemed now to welcome whatever responsibility might lie ahead.

She was still shabby, still small. But she no longer looked like a waif of eleven, a lonely stray defying a hostile world. She looked instead like what she was—a girl of fourteen at home in her world, now that she had begun to learn the secret of what made it go around.